'Lydia, listen to me.

'When I'm with you, I'm just a man—as you are a woman. I don't think differently because I am the son of a sheikh. I don't act differently. I am just like any other man. When I do this…'

He bent his proud head and took her lips in a long, deep kiss that made her senses reel.

'I am a man kissing a woman—my woman. The woman who has stolen my soul from me—my mind—leaving me incapable of thinking of anything beyond her.'

This Amir was no longer the civilised, controlled man she had met just hours before, but a fierce, arrogant Bedouin warrior, with the heat of the desert in his veins, the burn of the sun in his eyes.

'Let me tempt you, sweetheart,' he murmured against her ear. 'Let me persuade you to stay and I promise you'll never forget it. You can have anything you want. Everything you want…'

Kate Walker was born in Nottinghamshire, but as she grew up in Yorkshire she has always felt that her roots are there. She met her husband at university and originally worked as a children's librarian, but after the birth of her son she returned to her old childhood love of writing. When she's not working she divides her time between her family, their three cats, and her interests of embroidery, antiques, film and theatre, and, of course, reading.

You can visit Kate Walker's website at www.kate-walker.com or email her at kate@kate-walker.com

Recent titles by the same author:

HIS MIRACLE BABY
THE HOSTAGE BRIDE

DESERT
AFFAIR

BY
KATE WALKER

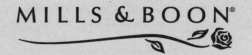

For Noelle, with love

First published in Great Britain 2001
Harlequin Mills & Boon Limited,
Eton House, 18-24 Paradise Road, Richmond, Surrey TW9 1SR

© Kate Walker 2001

ISBN 0 263 82572 8

Set in Times Roman 10½ on 11¼ pt.
01-0202-52561

Printed and bound in Spain
by Litografía Rosés, S.A., Barcelona

CHAPTER ONE

'EXCUSE me, but is this seat taken?'

Lydia didn't even have to look up to know who had spoken. There was only one person in the whole of the airport lounge who could have a voice like that. The sort of voice that wrapped itself around her senses like a slither of warmed silk, its low, lyrically accented tones making her skin shiver in reaction to the sheer sensuality of their sound.

She had spotted him as soon as she had walked into the room. It had been impossible *not* to notice him. He was tall, dark and devastatingly imposing; it seemed as if he were the only person in the place. The sort of man who would draw any woman's gaze with the automatic ease of a powerful magnet and then lazily hold onto it without any sort of effort on his part.

And he had made no effort at all. Though he could not have been unaware of her attention, the overwhelming interest she hadn't even had the strength to hide, he had done nothing at all to sustain it or show that it mattered in the slightest to him. No trace of reaction had touched the carved male beauty of his tanned face, no flicker of a smile either of welcome or even disdain. But he had not been unaware of her.

'I said...'

'I know what you said!'

The faint rasp of an edge to the beautiful voice, the hint of angry reproof, had her lifting her head sharply, tossing back the soft brown curls that framed her heart-shaped face. Wide-set blue eyes fringed by long, curling lashes clashed abruptly with harder, glittering black, and for a second she felt as if her heart had actually stopped in stunned disbelief.

Dear God, but he was even more spectacular close up! The true beauty of that golden skin, the sculpted cheek-bones and wide, hard, sensual slash of a mouth was like a blow in the pit of her stomach. His nose was long and straight, his hair unredeemed black, cut in an uncompro-misingly severe crop that emphasised the total perfection of the superb, clean-cut lines of his features.

And if he had seemed tall from a distance then standing over her like this, with those amazing eyes fixed search-ingly on her face, his impact was positively earth-shattering.

'I know what you said...'

Hastily Lydia adjusted her tone a degree or two down-wards, from the pitch to which shock and apprehension had pushed it, wishing she could erase the flaring wash of colour from her cheeks as easily.

'But I would have thought that it was obvious that no one was sitting there.'

And that no one had occupied the chair beside her for all of the—what? Almost three quarters of an hour since she had taken up her position here. After all, he had been watching her for almost all of that time.

She had tried to bury her face in the copy of the mag-azine she had bought to while away the time waiting for her flight to be called, but she had felt the burn of his brazen gaze fixed on her. And she had met its cold scrutiny head-on if she'd so much as glanced upwards from the page.

'I wondered if you might be waiting for someone.'

'Well, no, I'm not! I'm here on my own!'

'Then may I join you?'

'Why?'

She knew she sounded suspicious, as stiff as a cat being threatened by the approach of a stranger into its territory, but she couldn't help it. It was how she felt, wary and unsure of herself. If anything, *she* felt like the intruder into the luxurious, opulent surroundings of the VIP lounge. It was not the sort of place she normally frequented, not the sort of place she could ever have afforded to be in if it hadn't been for her new job, the generosity of her employers.

He, on the other hand, looked totally, supremely at home here. His long, lean body might be clothed in the same casual jeans and a jumper that she had chosen for practicality during a long flight, but there could be no doubt that his clothing was very definitely not from the chain store where she had bought hers. No, the lines of his clothing murmured of designer labels and expensive tailoring, and she was sure that the smoky grey sweater that hugged the firm lines of his chest and skimmed the narrow waist and hips could only be of the finest, softest cashmere available. Everything about him said Money, with a capital M.

And in spite of the supremely civilised nature of his appearance, something about him seemed to whisper of a wilder spirit, an untamed, elemental part of his character that didn't fit with the ultra-modern surroundings.

'Why?'

He shrugged indolent shoulders, unconsciously drawing attention to their width and strength.

'To while away a little time. To ease the boredom of waiting with some conversation.'

A tiny hint of a smile curled that devastating mouth up at one corner and the onyx eyes gleamed for a second with a hint of mocking amusement.

'Is that such a terrible idea?'

'N-no...'

This was even worse! Her tongue seemed to be tangling up on itself, refusing to get the words out in any coherent form, and she was stumbling over the simplest of answers. And it was not a sensation she was used to.

She didn't normally have this sort of trouble in talking to strangers. She was *trained* to talk to them, after all! Trained to handle almost any sort of eventuality or problem. So why did this one man affect her like this?

'I'm expecting my flight to be called at any minute.'

'I doubt it.'

His glance towards the huge plate-glass windows was wry, his mouth taking on an expressive twist as he surveyed the scene outside.

'The snow is definitely getting worse and the wind's picking up. It's blowing a blizzard out there. No pilot worth his salt is going to even think of taking off in conditions like this. You'll be lucky if you're only delayed by a couple of hours.'

'*Only* delayed,' Lydia echoed bleakly. 'As opposed to what?'

'To your flight being cancelled completely and the airport being shut down for today. I think you'd better consider that possibility...' he added, seeing the way her face fell. 'From what I can see, it can only get worse, not better.'

And what would she do then? Lydia was forced to wonder. If the airport closed, she had nowhere to go; nothing to go back to. Today was to have been the start of her new life, a whole new beginning.

'Would having a drink with me be such a bad thing?' The thread of irony was definitely darker now, making her shiver faintly just to hear it.

'No...'

But still she couldn't make herself say yes, please sit down, introduce herself. All the normal politeness and pleasantries seemed to have fled from her mind, leaving it shockingly blank as a wiped blackboard.

'Just what is it that you're afraid of?'

Silkily spoken though they were, she knew the words were meant to sting and they did. Sharply.

'Do you really think that I'm about to pounce on you in front of all these other passengers—not to mention the airport staff? Perhaps you fear that, driven mad by your stunning beauty, I will ravish you without mercy.'

'Oh, now you're just being ridiculous.'

She struggled to ignore the sudden twist of her heart, the judder in her pulse as the impact of that 'stunning beauty' hit home. His tone had been ironical but something deep in those spectacular eyes had told her that the words had been more seriously meant.

'Please don't be silly. It's just that...that I really don't see exactly why you should want to. What would you get from talking to a complete stranger who is due to head out of here on a plane at any minute? I mean...why me?' she ended on an uncharacteristically plaintive note.

The wordless sound he made with his tongue was sharp, impatient, speaking eloquently of the irritation and temper he was struggling to rein back. It was also totally un-English making her wonder just what his nationality might be. That accent certainly wasn't Italian or Spanish. It was far more exotic than that, in spite of impeccable pronunciation and a natural ease of grammar. There was an arrogance and pride in both his profile and his bearing that made her think fleetingly of long-ago kings or Bedouin warriors, but such fanciful thoughts flew from her head when he spoke again.

'You are clearly not a fool,' he declared with a sudden harshness that brought a gasp of shock to her lips. 'So why do you behave as if you were? You know very well what is between us—what has been there from the moment I first laid eyes on you and you on me.'

'No, I don't!'

Sitting down kept her too far beneath him, making her position too vulnerable for her liking. In a rush she started to her feet, only to find that instead of making things easier she had in fact made them much, much worse.

Face to face like this, on the same level at last, she was supremely conscious of the difference in their builds. At five feet ten inches, she had always considered herself overly tall for a woman, but this man had the rare ability to make her feel small.

His head and shoulders topped hers by several inches, and she found that unless she looked upwards at an awkward angle she was forced to focus on the dangerous sensuality of his mouth. His beautiful mouth and the smooth olive skin that surrounded it, faintly shadowed by several hours' growth of beard. Immediately her thoughts jumped to imagine just what it would feel like to have that mouth on hers, to press her own lips against the satin warmth of his face.

She was now so close to him that the clean, faintly musky scent of his body tantalised her senses. It was impossible not to inhale secretly, sparking a reaction like the internal prickle of pins and needles.

'I don't!' she repeated, less certainly this time. 'What do you mean what there is between us? I don't know what you are talking about.'

Black eyes flashed as he turned a look of pure scorn on her flushed face.

'You know only too well what I'm talking about,' he tossed back at her in a low, dangerous voice. 'We both know what is happening between us, even if you are too craven to admit to it and give it a name.'

Unexpectedly he leaned forwards, reaching out with one long, tanned hand. The tip of his finger touched her cheek very lightly and then moved slowly and caressingly downwards, etching a trail of fire along her skin.

'And it is a very simple word,' he murmured beguilingly. 'Short, to the point, and so easy to say if you only have the courage to trust in yourself.'

His eyes held her, keeping her transfixed, unable to move, unable to blink. And what she read in that steady, ebony gaze, the fierce flames that burned in the darkness of his pupils, gave her the answer she both wanted and dreaded.

Sex.

The word flared in Lydia's mind, etched in letters of white-hot flame, so that she was sure that this disturbing stranger must be able to look deep into her eyes and read it clearly there.

Sex.

Pure and undiluted. Primal. Powerful. Totally primitive. The sort of instinctive, unthinking response that couldn't be understood or explained. Human interaction at its most basic. It couldn't be denied and it couldn't be resisted.

That was what blazed between them. What had sparked in her senses in the first moment she had set eyes on this man when she had walked into the room.

And it was clear that he too had felt that same shock of carnal recognition, the body-blow to the soul that said, I *want* this person. I want them so much that I feel I will die if I never have them. It dried her throat and made her heart pound. Her clenched hands were damp with sweat, her lips parched, but she didn't dare do anything to ease either physical sensation. To do so would be to reveal to those watchful, hunting hawk's eyes that she was light years away from being as calm as she wanted to pretend.

'I...'

She opened her mouth to deny the accusation of cowardice, but the knowledge of the truth dried the protest on her tongue and turned it into a raw, embarrassing croak.

'You...?' he encouraged softly, the single, husky word a seduction in itself. And the spot where his fingertip still rested on her cheek was a burning focus, a concentration of all the sensations he aroused in her.

It seemed obscene to be at the mercy of such primitive feelings in such public, impersonal surroundings. All around her was the hushed murmur of voices in desultory conversation. Other passengers lounged in the comfortable chairs, turning the pages of newspapers and magazines, or frowned into laptop computers, occasionally leaning forward to touch a key. No one even spared them as much as a curious glance.

And yet Lydia had the feeling that the awareness that pulsed between her and this man—a man whose name she didn't even know—must have enclosed them in a glowing, burning haze that swirled in the air and coiled round them like smoke. Her heart was beating a frantic tattoo, and she was sure that the hard, strong finger must feel the race of the blood in her veins and know what had caused it.

'You...?' he prompted again, but her tongue seemed too thick, too frozen to speak, and she could only shake her head in numb confusion.

His reaction was brusque and startling, making her flinch in a moment of shocked panic. The long forefinger was snatched away with a swiftly muttered imprecation in some language she didn't know, the words too harsh and swift to catch. Then his hand came down in a violent, slashing movement between their two bodies as if he were cutting off all communication between them.

'Enough!' he declared in a voice that rang with cold anger. 'I do not have time for this...'

And before she could register exactly what he had in mind he had spun on his heel and was clearly about to march away from her, dismissing her totally from his mind.

'I...'

Lydia struggled with the tangle of feelings that had knotted high up in her throat, choking off speech.

'I...' she tried again, her voice croaking rawly. 'I... Oh, please! *Wait!*'

In her mind, the last word was a wild, desperate cry, one that would have brought confused, irritated, and just plain curious looks her way from every other waiting passenger. But what actually came out was a weak, uncertain whisper, one that broke in the middle.

And one that she was sure he couldn't have heard. It seemed that way at first because for the space of several jolting heartbeats he didn't seem to react. He certainly didn't pause, and the impetus of his anger was such that the force of his movement took him well away from her, almost into the middle of the room, before he came to an abrupt halt and slowly, very, very slowly, turned back to face her again.

'What did you say?'

'I said…'

Lydia swallowed hard because she wanted this to sound so very different from that first, frantic call.

'I said, please wait. Please don't go.'

One jet-black brow lifted in sardonic interrogation and his handsome head inclined slightly to one side in apparent thoughtful consideration of the situation.

'You've changed your mind?'

'I—changed my mind.'

Better to let him think that. Better to let him believe that she had had second thoughts than to let him know what *she* had known all along. That there was no way she could have let him just walk out of her life as suddenly as he had walked into it.

But it had been only when he had actually moved away from her and her heart had cried out in distress at being abandoned like this that she had realised how much she had wanted him to stay.

'You changed your mind—and you want—what?'

'I'd like you to stay. And talk…'

Still he didn't move.

'And perhaps have that drink you suggested. After all…'

She tried for an airy tone, waved a hand in the direction of the windows against which the snow now swirled in

wild, blustering eddies, the view of the runways, the waiting planes totally obliterated from sight.

'Clearly neither of us is going anywhere soon. We might
as well spend the time here together as apart. The hours
always drag so much when you're waiting.'

Her voice faltered, going up and down embarrassingly
as she stared into his stony, set face and met no response.

Was the man waiting for her to *beg*? She wouldn't! She
had more pride! And yet if he turned away again...

'Please won't you join me?'

Still he waited one more nicely calculated minute. Just
long enough to stretch out her screaming nerves even
more, to twist them into hard, painful knots of tension.
Then as suddenly as he had turned away he swung back,
covering the short distance between them in a few swift,
confident strides.

It was like seeing a sleek black panther coming towards
her, Lydia thought, struggling to push away uneasy visions
of herself as the prey and this man very definitely in the
role of predator.

But then he turned on her a smile of such supercharged
charm that it would have melted an iceberg. One that left
her feeling as if the weak, ineffectual barriers she had been
trying to build up against him had shattered into splinters,
falling hopelessly at her feet.

'I'm glad you changed your mind,' he said, the unexpected warmth of his tone so unlike the icy harshness of
moments before that it rocked her sense of reality, making
her wonder for a second if she was even talking to the
same man. 'I *hate* waiting. I have no patience at all.'

'Me too,' Lydia admitted. 'I was bored out of my head
already. And it looks as if we're in for a long delay. Do
you think any of those planes are going anywhere today?'

The glance he turned in the direction she indicated was
brief to the point of indifference and her heart jumped on

a thrill of delighted confusion as his ebony gaze came back to her face and fastened on it fixedly.

'I doubt it.'

His shrug dismissed the matter from his thoughts, his obvious lack of concern intensely gratifying to her uncertain self-esteem. After long, lonely months of feeling unwanted and rejected, the glow of appreciation that burned like fiery coals deep in the darkness of his eyes was a balm to her wounded pride.

'But it is no matter. We won't care how long we have to wait. We won't notice the time.'

'No...'

It was all she could manage because it was happening again. The warm sensuality of his tone had dried her throat, leaving her lips parched so that she had to slide her tongue over them to ease the discomfort. And as she saw that intent, black gaze drop to follow the small betraying movement she felt its force as if it were an actual touch on her skin, and shivered secretly in response.

The need for that touch to be a reality sent a wave of hunger through her that drained the strength from her legs so that she had to sink down suddenly onto the nearest chair. It was either that or give herself away completely by falling in a ridiculously weak heap right at his beautifully shod feet.

'Won't you sit down too?' she managed.

And it was as he came down beside her that a new feeling hit. A disturbing, scary sensation that made her feel as if something wet and icy had slowly slithered down the sensitive length of her spine.

She was suddenly totally and inexplicably convinced that her life would never be the same again. That the whole of her future was bound up with this man and there was no way she could break free at all.

CHAPTER TWO

'SO, WHAT shall we talk about?'

Lydia had to force herself to drag her thoughts back
from the disturbing paths they were determined to follow.
She had already let this man rattle her far too easily. It
was time she got back in control of the situation! Seeing
him as the ruler of her fate, indeed! He was just a new
acquaintance. A stunning, fascinating, lethally good-
looking one, admittedly, but just a man for all that.

But then her eyes met the dark, deep set ones of the
man beside her and the description 'just a man' once more
became totally inadequate.

'Where should we begin?'

'Names would be a good place to start.'

She aimed for crisp matter-of-factness and was pleased
to note that she actually managed to come close.

'We haven't even introduced ourselves yet. I'm Lydia
Ashton.'

She held out her hand as she spoke, feeling better now
that things were back on a more regular footing.

'And you are?'

A worrying glint of something that looked like amusement gleamed in his eyes but he followed her lead impec-
cably.

'Amir Zaman,' he said in that beautiful voice, the slight
accent deepening on the words.

'Amir…'

This was the normal path of things—meetings, intro-
ductions, getting to know someone… Then, and only then,
did you start to harbour the sort of unexpurgated, X-rated

thoughts that had been running wild in her head from the moment she had first set eyes on this man.

But then he took her hand in his and immediately she lost her grip on herself, all her careful control shattering in the space of a second.

His hand was warm and firm, his grip strong, controlled, she suspected, to ensure that the full force of it didn't crush her slighter fingers. But it was the feel of his flesh against hers, the sensual caress of skin against skin that sent a sensation like a fierce electrical charge shooting through her body. She had the crazy feeling that this was the one touch she had been waiting for all her life, and her head swam with the impact of its effect on her.

'Amir...' she tried again, struggling to conceal from him the way she was feeling. 'Unusual—and very definitely not English.'

'It's Arabic.' There was a surprising edge to his voice. 'It means Prince.'

It suited him too. Suited the proud carriage, the beautifully carved features, the way that dark head was held so arrogantly high. She could just imagine him in the wild, flowing robes of the Bedouin warriors. He would look stunning, exotic and magnificent.

'At least it means something. I once looked up Lydia in a dictionary of names. All it means, apparently, is ''a woman from Lydia'' which is somewhere in Greece.'

He was still holding her hand, she realised, not having released it after that first greeting. For the life of her she couldn't think of a way of freeing herself without communicating the wrong message with her actions.

So she simply let it lie where it was. Which was, after all, what she really wanted to do.

'Arabic.' Backtracking hastily, she tried to keep the conversation going. 'Is that where you're going?'

'To the Gulf?' The dark head inclined in agreement. 'That's where I was supposed to be flying to today.'

'You have friends there?'

'Family.'

Something had changed. Without knowing how, she had blundered in on a subject he didn't want to talk about, innocently crashing through barriers that she hadn't realised were there. There was a new hardness in the brilliant eyes, tightness around his mouth and jaw that made her shiver faintly in unease.

Perhaps it was the fact of being in a VIP lounge for the first—and probably the only—time in her life. Or perhaps it had something to do with being in transit, so to speak, not actually belonging anywhere at all at the moment, but being partway between her old life and the new. That and the whirling snow outside, obliterating the safe, familiar world she knew, had given her a strange sense of unreality. It was as if this room, this space where she and Amir Zaman sat, had become a separate little enclosed universe, a bubble suspended out of time, where none of the rules by which she normally ran her life actually worked, or even mattered.

Suddenly his hold on her hand no longer seemed so comfortable or so welcome. With a slight tug she managed to loosen his grasp, ease herself free.

'I think I'd like something to drink,' she managed unevenly.

'Of course.'

In an instant the disturbingly distant mood had vanished and he was all attention, all concern, the jet eyes turning immediately in search of an attendant.

One look was all it took. He didn't even raise his hand, made no gesture at all that she could detect, and yet the girl in the airport uniform immediately headed in their direction, summoned by the silent command.

'Yes, sir? What can I get for you?'

'Lydia? What would you like? Coffee? Or perhaps some wine?'

'Just coffee, please,' Lydia responded hastily. She didn't dare risk anything alcoholic. She was intoxicated enough as it was.

'Coffee for two, then.'

'Yes, sir.'

Lydia would not have been surprised to see her actually bob a respectful curtsey. The tone of his voice was pitched just right. It was perfectly polite, even courteous, but there was a note in it that demanded instant and total obedience, and warned of the risk of possible repercussions if that compliance was not forthcoming.

Obviously this Amir Zaman was someone who was used to giving orders—and having those orders carried out, she thought, studying the handsome face even more closely. And Amir meant Prince...

'Lydia...?'

'I—I'm sorry... What was it you said?'

Did he suspect that her thoughts had been of him? Of course he did! He did more than suspect. He *knew*. And it pleased him. Because it was what he wanted.

'I asked where you were travelling to. Where did you plan on flying to today if the weather had not intervened?'

'Oh—I was going to America. To California.'

And America was in the opposite direction to the way he was going. Fate had brought them together like this, but only for the briefest moment. And before very long fate would take them even further apart than ever.

She was going to America. Amir was stunned to find how much that fact affected him. It seemed to have the kick of a mule right in his stomach.

And why? Because this woman was heading in the opposite direction to him? Because she was going to California while he had to be in Kuimar?

'What's in California? A man?'

He tried to keep the question light, to reveal nothing of

the knot that formed in his stomach and pulled tight at just the thought of her with someone else.

'No, not a man—a job! *The* job. The sort of position I've been looking for for years. A dream job. Have you heard of the Halgrave Group of hotels.'

'I know of them.'

Of course he knew of them, Lydia reflected. Anyone with the sort of money he obviously had would know of the worldwide chain of exclusive, sinfully expensive hotels that had its base in California and a branch in almost every capital of the world.

'Well, they actually head-hunted me. I was working as Hospitality Manager in a Leicester hotel and they—they heard of me! They rang me up and asked me to come to a specially arranged interview. They offered me a position right there and then.'

'In California?'

'In California to start with. I have to do a six-week course to learn more about the company—the way they do things. After that I could be sent anywhere—anywhere at all. The world's my oyster.'

And the offer of a job couldn't have come at a better time. With her relationship with Jonathon floundering on the rocks, her dreams of becoming Mrs Lydia Carey totally shattered, she had been in desperate need of something to put in their place. When Halgrave had asked if she was prepared to travel, she had practically bitten their hand off in her eagerness.

And she wouldn't be human if she hadn't found herself wishing that Jon had known about her new venture. He had always accused her of being too conservative, too cautious.

'You're so careful about everything it's downright boring, Lydia,' he had scorned. 'No one would believe you're not even twenty-five yet, you're such an old stick-in-the-mud!'

And clearly Jon hadn't wanted to be married to a stick-in-the-mud, she reflected bitterly.

The return of the waitress with their drinks provided a much-needed diversion, a chance for her to recollect her thoughts and bring them back into the present, pushing away the discomfort of her memories of the past.

'How do you like your coffee?' Amir asked, taking control of even this small matter.

'Lots of milk, no sugar.'

He took his exactly the opposite way, she noticed, totally black and sweet. But it was the swift, efficient movements of his hands that fascinated her, the stunning effect of dark, luxuriant eyelashes lying in sooty arcs above the slashing cheekbones as he looked down to focus on the simple task.

He couldn't be more opposite to Jonathon either, she couldn't help reflecting. The other man had such a very English complexion, combined with smooth blond hair and blue eyes. The sort of colouring that she would have said was much more her type. Which was why it was so surprising that Amir had had this shockingly powerful effect on her.

'So there's no one you're leaving behind?' Amir continued the conversation where they had left off at the waitress' arrival. 'No one you'll miss?'

'No. Not even my parents. My parents decided to take a redundancy package that Dad was offered and went out to live in Portugal—opening a bar there. So, as I'm an only child, there was nothing to keep me here. No one to stay for.'

'And what if I were to ask you to stay?'

'What?'

Hastily swallowing down the sip of coffee that now threatened to choke her, Lydia set her cup and saucer on the table with a distinct crash. Looking into his darkly

handsome face, she searched for the look of irony, the hint
of amusement that would tell her he had only been joking.

She found none. Instead, her disbelieving look was met
with one of total composure. And every evidence of total
sincerity.

'W-what did you say?'

That black-eyed gaze didn't falter but held her wide-
eyed look with an intent force that dried her mouth and
set her heart fluttering high up in her throat.

'You know only too well what I said. And, what's more,
you know exactly why I said it.'

'No—I...'

She looked like a startled fawn when she stared at him
like that, Amir found himself thinking. Or like one of the
newborn foals that were such a delight to him as they
stared around, huge, stunned eyes trying to make sense of
this new world into which they had arrived.

'It's quite simple,' he told her softly, leaning forward
so that the husky whisper would reach her ears—and her
ears alone. 'I have this fantasy that you do not get on that
plane to California this afternoon. That you do not fly off
to America and this wonderful new job...'

Her head went back sharply, blue eyes widening even
more, her lips parting on a faint gasp of shock. He let his
smile soothe her as he reached out slowly and gently. He
caught her chin, resting one long finger and a thumb on
either side, holding her still with only the lightest of pres-
sure.

'But instead, in my dream, you stay here with me, and
we explore what we've discovered. See where this takes
us.'

'We...'

Lydia couldn't force her tongue around another word.
Her thoughts were a whirling mass of chaos, incapable of
forming a single coherent thread. The only thing she knew
or recognised was this man before her. This hard-boned,

devastating face, the obsidian glitter of those deep eyes holding hers with hypnotic ease.

And because her gaze was fixed on him so intently she saw the tiny flicker of a change when it came. Saw it, and knew what it meant, but her mind was too numb to react or pull away. Besides, she knew that she didn't *want* to react. That she wouldn't have freed herself even if she could, for all that his hold on her chin was so gentle it could have been broken in a second.

So she stayed where she was. Stayed absolutely still and watched that dark head come closer. Watched the devastating mouth soften, and come down on her own lips with obvious intent.

And that was when she realised that the softness had been deceptive. That his kiss was not the light, enticing caress she had been anticipating. Instead it was firm and strong and forceful, a revelation of feeling and a statement of intent all in one. In the same moment that it seemed to cajole her soul out of her body, it also awoke every stinging sense with the burn of a promise that made her thoughts swim in a heady delirium of longing.

And all the time he hadn't touched her except with his mouth. That long, strong body was still held well away from her, even the hand under her chin releasing her and falling back to his side, the other still resting on the strong, muscular thigh under the denim jeans.

He didn't need to hold her, and he knew it. Lydia knew it too. Knew that it was as much the force of her own feelings as anything he did that kept her in her seat, unable to move. That the flickers of white hot flame along every nerve in her body seemed to melt her bones, leaving her unable to support herself if she so much as tried to stand up.

'Help me, Lydia,' Amir murmured against her lips. 'Tell me what I can do to make you stay. To keep you by my side for just a little while longer.'

'I...'

Could she be hearing right? Had this stunning man actually said that he wanted her to stay? And was it possible that she was actually considering saying yes? She hardly knew any more about him than his name. She had no idea if she could trust him in any way.

Bewildered, she could only shake her head in bemusement at her own reaction.

'No?'

Amir had mistaken the reason for her reaction.

'Then let me persuade you...'

This time his kiss was pure enticement. Gently he edged her lips open, let the tip of his tongue play along their sensitised surface, making her sigh aloud in response. And now at last he moved, powerful fingers tangling in the soft fall of her hair, closing over the fine bones of her skull, holding her still so that he could deepen and prolong the caress.

Lydia's whole being was awash with a golden heat. Her heart was racing, pounding the blood through her veins and making her thoughts swim in sensuous reaction. She was lost, she knew, drowning in sensation, a wild need uncoiling deep inside her, centring hotly at the point between her thighs.

'Amir...'

'Ladies and gentlemen...'

A new sound intruded on the delirious yearning that hazed her mind. A man's voice, crisp and matter-of-fact and hatefully jarring in the way it broke into her sense of isolation, jolting her back to reality with a suddenness that shattered her sensual mood.

'Ladies and gentlemen, your attention please. We regret to inform you...'

The rest of the words passed totally over Lydia's head. Her brain seemed to have blown a fuse and she was incapable of taking anything in. Even the simplest words

failed to make the slightest sense and when the announcement was over she could only stare blankly at Amir, her
light brown brows drawing together in dazed confusion.

'What was all that about? What did they mean all services are cancelled?'

'I did warn you.' Amir's tone was dry. 'The weather
has been getting worse all day. The blizzard's closed in
and no planes can take off or land tonight. There'll be no
flights out of here at least until tomorrow morning—if
then.'

'No flights!' Lydia echoed, horror etched into her face.
'But why—how? Did you…?'

For a second she actually believed he might have been
able to arrange it.

Amir's laughter should have reassured her, but somehow it had exactly the opposite result.

'My sweet Lydia, do you really think that I am capable
of that? To organise such a thing I would have had to enter
into a pact with the Almighty—or perhaps the Devil.'

Now *that* she could believe, Lydia admitted to herself.
The wicked curl to his lips, the look of triumph in those
eyes could only be described as fiendish. He might not
have been able to arrange this situation, but it was quite
clear that he fully intended to benefit from it. And his next
words confirmed as much.

'But, no matter who created this, they have my undying
gratitude. Now you'll have to stay.'

'But I can't stay here!'

Lydia's brain was working overtime, struggling to as-
sess the situation, sort it out in her thoughts and come up
with a solution.

'Where can I go? Where will I sleep?'

Oh, if only she hadn't given up her hotel room this
morning! But she had left Leicester yesterday full of hope
and excitement, looking forward to a totally fresh start.
She had only booked for an overnight stay because she

had always thought that by now she would be in her seat on board the plane, heading away from England and towards the new life she had dreamed of.

'What do I do now?'

'Don't panic,' Amir soothed. 'You can…'

Abruptly he caught himself up. What in hell's name was he doing? Had he really been intending to offer her the chance to stay in the apartment? Was he out of his mind?

It seemed he was. That was the only conclusion he could draw from the way he had behaved ever since he had first set eyes on this Lydia Ashton when she had walked into the room barely a couple of hours ago. His brain had to have been completely scrambled for him to have behaved as he had!

'…in my dream, you stay here with me, and we explore what we've discovered. See where this takes us.'

Had he really said that? Had he really been such a total, complete fool?

What was wrong with him?

Oh, he fancied this woman; there was no denying that. He most definitely had the hots for her—and how! But was he such a fool as to be led by his hormones into making what could possibly be the most dreadful mistake? Very likely the worst possible mistake of his life?

So this Lydia appealed to his most basic instincts. He had only to look at her to want her in his bed, that soft mouth opening under his, the fine curves of her body crushed close to his own frame, the bronze silk of her hair tangling around his fingers. Even now, just to think of it made him ache in such intensity that he wanted to groan out loud.

But how much was he prepared to pay for one night of passion—for the quick, urgent appeasement of his most masculine needs, the scratching of an itch, which was really all that this one-night stand would amount to?

Would this woman—any woman—be worth the sacrifice of all that he had worked towards for so long? Was any sexual gratification, however intense—and every instinct told him that with her it would be the most intense pleasure of his life—worth the loss of his lifetime's ambition? Could he really just abandon the goal towards which he had worked for the last twenty years, ever since the day of his eleventh birthday, when his mother had told him the truth about his father and his heritage?

No!

With an abruptness that jarred Lydia right to her soul, he suddenly released her and pushed himself sharply to his feet.

'You can find a hotel room to stay in overnight. The airline will have provided accommodation for everyone. If you come with me...'

He had already turned on his heel and marched off before Lydia had the time to collect her thoughts and gather up her magazine and her hand luggage. She could only stare bemusedly after him as she struggled to her feet, the sharp sting of distress adding to her mental confusion.

What had she done or said to make him react like this? Why had his mood changed so abruptly? Only moments before she had been sure that he had been about to offer her somewhere to stay the night with him.

And that if he had, she had been about to accept it.

But she had to have been deluding herself. She didn't even know if he lived in London, let alone close enough to get to tonight.

Face it, Lydia, she told herself in fierce reproof as she headed after Amir, you don't know enough about him to agree to *anything*. Coffee was okay. Letting him kiss you, bad enough. And as for 'in my dream, you stay here with me, and we explore what we've discovered'—you weren't really going to go along with that—*were you*?

'It's all sorted.'

Amir was heading back to her, making his way through the buzzing crowd with elegant ease.

'They're ringing round all the airport hotels now. You just have to wait and they'll let you know which one they're putting you in.'

'Great!'

She tried to make it enthusiastic and hoped it sounded better in his ears than it did in her own. She should be feeling relieved. Very possibly she had just had an extremely narrow escape.

But relieved didn't describe her mood at all. Instead she felt as limp as a pricked balloon.

'What about you?'

'Oh, I'll head back to my apartment. The snow may be bad but I should get there okay.'

One tanned hand lifted, revealing a slim, silver mobile phone.

'I just called my driver. He's bringing the car round right away.'

Was he really as keen to leave her as that? 'He's bringing the car round *right away*.' So much for 'you stay here with me'. He hadn't even waited to see her into a taxi, heading for her hotel. And as he spoke he was moving, drifting over to the huge windows, obviously intent on looking out to see if his car had arrived yet.

'So this is goodbye?' The words sounded bleak, desperately final.

'I guess it is.'

Another couple of minutes, Amir told himself. Just sixty—a hundred or so—seconds, and she would be gone. On her way to the hotel and out of his life. He could put her out of his mind, and maybe tomorrow when he woke up he'd be thankful that he hadn't given into the carnal temptation that had distorted his thinking so badly.

Just another sixty seconds…but they seemed to be ticking away far too slowly. And instead of feeling thankful, the only thoughts in his head were of just how lovely she looked standing there, with the soft bronze hair tumbled around her shoulders, her blue eyes wide and clear. The cream-coloured wool of her sweater clung in all the right places, the tight denim of her jeans hugging the curving hips and neat bottom with sensual provocation.

Seeing how the fullness of her mouth had been kissed free of lipstick, he found it impossible not to recall that *he* had done that and he had enjoyed every second of the experience. He still had the taste of her on his lips and his tongue. If he was honest he wanted her mouth again, wanted the...

No! Furiously he drew himself up, ruthlessly reining in the hunger that threatened to escape even his determined control. Out of the corner of his eye he saw the sleek dark shape of the Jaguar on the road below, edging its way through the whirling snowflakes, towards the entrance. Nabil had wasted no time.

'It's been a pleasure meeting you.'

'And you,' Lydia managed, matching his stiff withdrawal tone for tone.

To her total consternation hot tears were burning in her eyes and she blinked them back desperately, refusing to let them fall. He had already left her, mentally at least. There was no point in hanging around, dragging this out painfully. Far better to get it over and done with. Short and sharp, like ripping a sticking plaster off a wound in the hope that that way it would hurt much less.

'Goodbye, then.'

'Goodbye, Lydia.'

Why was she still hanging about? Over on the other side of the room someone was making an announcement about the rooms that were being provided, reading out names from a long list. When the idea of listening and learning where she would be tonight slid into Amir's mind he crushed it down immediately, refusing to let it take root.

Lydia Ashton was a complication he could do without. He didn't have room for her—or for any other woman in his life right now. Dammit, he was as good as married, at least in his father's eyes, if not in his own.

Unfortunately his body was refusing to obey his mind. Just being near to this woman was enough to make his heart beat in double-quick time, his blood throb in his veins. Rationally he might accept that she was trouble, but the more basic instinctive response that tightened every nerve, fanned the embers of hunger into a blazing, roaring flame, declared that it was a trouble he would welcome into his life. Every second that she hesitated was wearing down his resistance, reducing his will to fight.

'See you...'

At last she was turning away. Just as he thought he was home and free, just as he foolishly let his guard down a second too early, she suddenly swung back. He saw what was coming and was powerless to prevent it.

Her lips were on his cheek, warm and soft and delicately caressing. The soft curves of her body were pressed against his, her breasts against the wall of his chest, his pelvis cradling the finer bones of hers. A delicate perfume of lily and rose seemed to envelop him in a cloud, and underneath it was the clean, subtle scent of her skin, sweet and potent in a way that made his head spin dangerously.

'Lydia...' he tried to protest, but his voice failed him.

And then as he turned his head her lips touched his and he knew that he was lost.

With a groan he gave up the fight that he had been losing anyway and hauled her up against him, crushing her hard, imprisoning her in the strength of his arms.

'Don't go, Lydia,' he muttered, the words rough and thick and raw. 'Don't go to the hotel. Come back with me to my apartment. Stay with me tonight.'

She should never have kissed him.

Lydia recognised her mistake in the second that she

made it, but she was powerless to stop herself, incapable of resisting the impulse. She had meant it to be just a quick peck on his cheek, the briefest touch, there and gone again in a moment, but it didn't quite work out like that.

The second she felt the warmth of his skin, tasted it against her mouth, she knew she was lost. Heat flooded her body, turning her brain to molten liquid and leaving her incapable of thought. Her breasts were crushed against the hardness of his chest, her hips clamped tight against his so that she could feel the hard, heated force of his desire for her before she heard the echo of it in his voice.

And when he turned his head and his lips took hers in hungry demand she knew she didn't have a prayer.

'Don't go, Lydia...' he said, but really they both knew she wasn't going anywhere at all.

There was no way she could stay in a hotel room tonight. No way she could endure the soulless emptiness of even the best five-star accommodation. Not without him.

'Stay with me tonight,' Amir muttered rawly against her mouth and on a deep, aching sigh of surrender she gave him the only answer she could think of.

'Yes,' she muttered, her voice every bit as rough and uneven as his had been. 'Yes, yes, *yes*! Of course I'll stay with you.'

CHAPTER THREE

'OH, WOW!'

Lydia didn't even try to hide her amazement as she turned in a slow, stunned circle, staring unreservedly at everything around her.

'This is just amazing! Is it really all yours?'

When Amir had spoken of his apartment, she had known from his clothes and the fact that he had been in the VIP lounge that he wouldn't live in a small, shabby couple of rooms like those she had just left behind in Leicester. And the sight of his car and the waiting uniformed driver who had leapt from his seat to open the door for them had increased that certainty one hundredfold. But she had never anticipated anything like *this*.

The huge penthouse apartment would have swallowed up her small flat twenty times or more and still had room to spare. The high ceilings and huge windows gave an impression of air and space, and beyond the plate glass the brilliant night skyline of London glittered even through the raging snowstorm. Rich furnishings, heavy silk brocaded curtains and thick, thick carpets in all the tones of gold from the palest clotted cream to a deep dark bronze meant that the room appeared warm and welcoming in spite of the unpleasantness of the night. And to add to the sense of comfort, a bright fire burned in the wide hearth.

'Actually it's my father's. His taste is rather more ornate than mine.'

The sweep of his hand indicated the enormous, brilliantly sparkling chandeliers, the marble fireplace.

'But I have the use of it when I'm in London.'

'And who is your father?' Lydia was intrigued.

The sudden change in his face told her that once more she'd overstepped those invisible barriers, an unnerving glint in his dark eyes warning her to back off—fast.

Behind them, a small, discreet cough alerted them to the silent, stocky figure of the chauffeur standing just inside the doorway, still holding Lydia's hand luggage, which he had carried up in the lift with them.

'Oh, thank you!' she said impulsively, moving to take it from him, but the man's attention was fixed on Amir.

'Will that be all, Highness?' he asked. 'Or is there anything more you will want tonight.'

'Nothing.' Amir's tone was dismissive. 'If the weather clears, I will need you to drive Miss Ashton back to the airport tomorrow, but I'll let you know about that. You can take the rest of the night off.'

Lydia watched in bemused disbelief as Nabil swept a low bow before backing towards the door. He had almost reached it when she suddenly thought of something.

'Oh, wait a moment, please...'

Hunting in her handbag, she pulled out her purse. But before she could open it, Amir's hand, swift and firm, had clamped down hard on hers, stilling her movement.

'You can leave, Nabil.'

Another bow and the man was gone. As the door swung to behind him, she turned to Amir, annoyance sparking in her sapphire eyes.

'I wanted to give him a tip!' she protested. 'He drove us here safely in the most appalling conditions. And he carried my bag up...'

The impetuous words faded from her lips as she saw Amir's dark, reproving frown, the obvious disapproval in his face.

'It is not appropriate,' he snapped, releasing her at last.

'Not appropriate...But why? Highness!' she recalled shakenly. 'He called you *Highness*!'

It sounded even more unbelievable spoken aloud in her own voice.

'And you…just who *is* your father? Who are *you*?'

Amir had moved to the opposite side of the room where an opened bottle of wine stood on a tray alongside a pair of the finest crystal wineglasses. Ignoring her questions, he poured a little into one of the goblets and tasted it carefully. Evidently it met with his approval because he swiftly filled both glasses and held one out to her, the ruby-coloured liquid glowing fiercely in the light of the fire.

'Would you like a drink?'

'What I'd *like* is an answer—preferably several!'

His irritated frown told her that her voice had been pitched too high. It had needed to be for her to hear it over the fearful pounding of her own heart. Her pulse was beating far too fast, making the blood sound like thunder inside her head.

'I want an explanation. For a start, just *who* is your father?'

His shrug dismissed her question as a minor irritation, much as he might have flicked away an annoyingly buzzing fly.

'My father's identity is not relevant to this situation.'

'Your father's identity is supremely *relevant*!' Lydia countered, her breath hissing in furiously through her teeth. 'Because, Your *Highness*…' she emphasised the word viciously '…if you don't give me an explanation of exactly who you are and what is happening, then I am out of here—fast.'

His smile was slow, mocking, filled with infuriating condescension.

'And where, exactly, would you go?' he drawled smoothly.

The truth was that she had no idea. She didn't even really know where in London they were. She had caught a glimpse of the wide flow of the Thames, the huge arc of the London Eye, the Houses of Parliament on the opposite bank, but apart from that she was lost. But she wasn't going to let him see that that worried her.

'I don't know and I don't care! But I know one thing—I won't stay here! Not unless you start telling me the truth.'

'The truth?'

Amir sipped his wine, savouring it appreciatively before he swallowed.

'The truth is simple. It's just you and I—a man and a woman who find each other attractive and want to be together. That is all there is to it. Are you sure you wouldn't like some of this wine? It really is excellent.'

Warily Lydia eyed the glass he held out to her again, a look of suspicion on her face.

'What is this, Amir? You wouldn't be trying to get me drunk, would you?'

The response she expected was that look of reproof once again, so she was thoroughly thrown off balance by the soft, warm sound of his laughter.

'And why would I do that, my dear Lydia? So that I can have my wicked way with you? I hardly think so. For one thing, my tastes don't run to a comatose partner, and for another, the way that you responded to me earlier, the fact that you are here with me now, would appear to indicate that I would not have to resort to such underhand methods to seduce you.'

'You might have other things in mind.'

'Such as?'

He looked deep into her stubbornly set face and his smile grew, that infuriatingly appealing chuckle sounding deep in his throat again.

'Oh, please—not the white slave trade as well! Lydia, sweetheart, you really must not let your imagination run away with you! I assure you, I have nothing but your comfort at heart. You have had a long, frustrating day stuck in that airport lounge, waiting for a flight that never came. I brought you here so that you could unwind and get some rest.'

'Fat chance of that...' Lydia began, but he ignored her furious interjection and continued imperturbably.

'I'm sure you must be hungry. Right now, my house-keeper will be preparing our meal. All you have to do is to have a drink and wait for it to be served.'

The mention of a housekeeper was unexpected and a relief. Simply knowing that she wasn't alone with him in the apartment eased some of the tension that had held Lydia so tight. The stiffness of her spine relaxed, her shoulders dropping slightly, her whole body loosening up.

'That's better.'

Amir smiled his approval.

'You no longer look as if you expect to be executed at any moment. Now, if you'll just have a drink...'

With an impatient sound in her throat, Lydia snatched at the glass. Perhaps the wine would relax her a little. Even if she wasn't as stiffly uptight as she had been before, her stomach was still twisting painfully.

'It is delicious,' she conceded ungraciously as she let a mouthful of the rich, mellow liquid slide down her disturbingly dry throat. 'But you needn't think I'm letting you get away with it. I still want some answers to my questions...'

Amir's sigh was a masterpiece, a perfect blend of irritation and resignation.

'And clearly you are not going to give me any peace until I answer them,' he drawled, lowering himself elegantly into one of the huge, soft armchairs and leaning back against the cushions, his long legs stretched out in front of him. 'All right, then, ask away—but at least make yourself comfortable first. You make me feel uneasy, hovering over me like an avenging angel.'

When Lydia was tempted to fling at him the comment that she didn't give a damn how she made him feel, she hastily thought the better of it. For one thing, she seriously doubted that anything she did would make this man uncomfortable. And for another, the brief, worryingly dangerous mood that Amir had displayed just moments ago now seemed to have passed. She didn't want to risk provoking him into letting it come to the surface again.

'All right,' she conceded grudgingly, coming to sit opposite him, on the other side of the fire.

The wine really was wonderful, she admitted to herself, taking another appreciative swallow. She had never tasted anything quite so delicious. It was clearly a million miles away from the sort of supermarket plonk that was all she could ever afford.

'So,' Amir prompted when, lulled by the alcohol and the warmth of the leaping flames in the deep hearth, she took her time about continuing the conversation, 'what exactly is it that you want to know?'

'You can start with explaining who your father is. He must be someone important. I mean, I've never met anyone at all who was given the title of "Highness".'

His sigh was less good-tempered this time. Clearly his patience was wearing thin again.

'Since you are so determined not to let the subject drop—my father's name is Sheikh Khalid bin Hamad Al Zaman, King of Kuimar.'

For once, something had shut her up, he thought wryly, watching the way her soft mouth fell slightly open on a gasp of surprise. She looked totally dumbfounded at the news, which was hardly surprising. He had had much the same response himself when he had first learned the truth. Though, being only eleven at the time, he had expressed his disbelief rather more forcefully.

'You're joking!'

'I'm totally serious, I assure you.'

'You're really the son of a sheikh?'

'Only just,' Amir returned obscurely.

'Oh!'

It was about all Lydia could manage. She was remembering how she had imagined him dressed in the dramatic robes of a desert warrior. The thought had her burying her nose in her wineglass and taking a hasty sip.

'So, should I be curtseying to you—calling you Highness, too?'

'Lydia!' Amir groaned reproachfully. 'That's not what I want from you.'

'What *do* you want?' The question wouldn't be held back.

The look he shot her from under hooded eyelids held a distinctly sexual challenge in it, polished ebony eyes gleaming behind luxuriantly curling lashes.

'You have to ask? I thought it was patently obvious. I thought we both understood where we stand...'

Lydia shifted uncomfortably under that wickedly taunting scrutiny, his gaze seeming to strip away a protective layer of skin, leaving her painfully vulnerable and exposed.

'I thought so too—at first.'

'So what has changed?'

Amir sipped at his wine again, his intent stare not moving from her flushed face.

'You don't need me to tell you that!' she protested furiously. 'You know what's changed! *You've* changed! Your father is a sheikh. And, correct me if I'm wrong, but doesn't that make you one too?'

The way that Amir's sensual mouth twisted sharply told her she had displeased him. For the space of an uncomfortable couple of heartbeats she was sure that he wasn't going to answer, but then abruptly he inclined his head in brusque agreement.

'If you want my full name it's Amir bin Khalid Al Zaman. *Sheikh* Amir bin Khalid Al Zaman,' he reiterated with an impenetrable intonation on the words. 'My father named me Crown Prince on my thirtieth birthday.'

'You see!' Lydia exclaimed. 'This changes everything. You're royalty! And I'm just a very ordinary girl who—'

She broke off sharply as, with a muttered curse, Amir suddenly slammed his glass down onto the table with such a distinct crash that she fully expected to see the delicate crystal shatter into a thousand glistening pieces. The next moment he was on his feet, covering the space between their chairs in two long, forceful strides.

'It doesn't matter!' he declared, his tone rough and hard. 'Can't you see? It doesn't matter a damn!'

Before Lydia could quite register what was happening, he had clamped hard fingers around the tops of her arms and hauled her up out of the chair with such force that she fell against him, her own hands going out frantically, desperately seeking support. Beneath her clutching fingers she felt the hard muscles bunch and tense as Amir took her weight.

'Who I am, or what I am, has no bearing on this situation.'

'No bearing…'

It was difficult to speak. Almost impossible to *think*. The strength of his arms was all that held her upright. The heat of his body seemed to reach out and enclose her, enfolding her in sensual warmth. And the clean, spicy scent of his skin coiled around her senses, tantalising her nostrils, reminding her of the burning kisses they had shared until she could almost taste him again on her tongue.

'But it has to! It has to change so much!'

'Lydia, listen to me.'

Amir gave her a small shake, not rough but just hard enough to break through the buzzing haze of response inside her head and draw her eyes to his face. The fierce emotions that she saw there transfixed her, holding her unable to look away, every ounce of her concentration centred on him.

'When I'm with you, there is just you and me. Nothing

else matters a damn. When I'm with you I'm just a man—as you are just a woman. We are simply male and female, Amir and Lydia. Money, position, our place in life, all become totally irrelevant. I don't think differently because I am the son of a sheikh. I don't act differently. I am just like any other man. When I do this…'

He bent his proud head and took her lips in a long, deep kiss that made her senses reel. The blood burned in her veins, melting away all resistance until she was pliant against him, every muscle weakening, her bones seeming to melt.

'I am a man kissing a woman—my woman. The woman I want to possess so much that I *ache* with it! The woman who has stolen my soul from me—my mind, leaving me incapable of thinking of anything beyond her.'

She was crushed even closer, pressed so hard up against him that she felt the burn of the swollen evidence of his desire and shivered in response. This Amir was no longer the civilised, controlled man she had met just hours before but a fierce, arrogant, Bedouin warrior, with the heat of the desert in his veins, the burn of the sun in his eyes.

'I shouldn't be here. We shouldn't be here. I…'

Abruptly he broke off as a light tap came at the door. Amir froze, muttered something roughly, then looked down into Lydia's stunned face, probing her eyes searchingly.

Apparently what he saw there satisfied whatever question was in his mind because he gave a swift, brusque nod and turned his head towards the door.

'Come!'

It was all command, pure autocrat, giving Lydia a swift insight into the other Amir, *Sheikh* Amir Al Zaman.

The middle-aged, dark-haired woman who came halfway across the threshold then paused, bobbing a hasty bow, clearly knew that man only too well. She kept her head bent, her eyes on the ground as Amir fired a question at her in a language Lydia could not understand. She answered in the same language, receiving a nod of approval for her pains, and was clearly thankful to be dismissed, almost scuttling away in her haste to be gone.

'Did you have to speak to her like that?' Lydia protested indignantly when they were alone again.

'Like what, precisely?' Amir enquired, looking down his long, straight nose at her.

'Ordering her about that way! She clearly couldn't wait to get out of here.'

'So you speak Arabic—and the Kuimar dialect?'

His mocking tone set her teeth on edge. He didn't have to tell her she had got things wrong. It was there in every inflexion, every word. Deciding discretion was the best policy, Lydia refused to let herself be provoked into rash speak and waited instead for him to explain, as she had no doubt that he was going to do.

'Jamila had come to tell us that the meal she has prepared is ready. Naturally, she was embarrassed at intruding on what she felt was a very private moment. I assured her that she was not to blame if my lady friend did not understand the conventions...'

Did he know how ambiguous he had made that 'lady friend' sound? Lydia wondered, irritation stinging sharply. She very much suspected that he did—and that it had been quite deliberate. Her teeth snapped shut as she bit off the angry retort she was tempted to make.

'I understand the conventions only too well,' she managed with a stiffly clenched jaw. The irony of the situation only added to her annoyance, Jonathon's accusation of being a stick-in-the-mud sounding sharply in her head.

'But not as Jamila sees them. In Kuimar, no respectable woman would be seen alone with a man in his home at night.'

'No respectable woman!' He was really intent on compounding the insulting effect of that 'lady friend.'

'We are not in Kuimar now.'

'No, we're not.'

The hint of a curl at the corners of Amir's carved mouth seemed to indicate that he was only too aware of the struggle she was having to keep her voice reasonable and that, infuriatingly, he found that distinctly amusing.

'Which is what I told Jamila before I gave her the rest of the night off. Are you hungry?'

'Am I…?'

Lydia found the question difficult to consider, and not just because of the speed with which Amir had jumped from one topic to another. The realisation that the house-keeper, whose presence had seemed such a comfort only a few minutes ago, had now been dismissed for the night put her into a distinctly uncomfortable state of mind. She would be alone with Amir after all, and alone with him in a way that 'no respectable woman' should ever be.

Shouldn't that be her cue to say that she'd changed her mind? That she couldn't stay here after all. That she found she actually preferred the thought of the hotel room so would he please send for Nabil, or a taxi, and she'd head straight back to the airport?

Except that, as she had just said, they weren't in Kuimar. And the truth was that, even if it was safer, more respect-able—more *sensible*—she didn't want to go.

Jonathon would never recognise her in the woman who knew she wanted to throw caution to the winds and stay here, ignoring every warning, every scream of self-preservation from the cautious 'stick-in-the-mud' part of her.

'Hungry? Yes, I'm starving!'

To her consternation, Amir met her response with a faint frown. One long finger touched her cheek as his beautiful mouth tightened disturbingly.

'Not the right answer, my dear Lydia.'

The thought of what the *right* answer should have been made her toes curl tightly inside her shoes.

'Not the right one, maybe.' She tried for laughter only to find that it broke revealingly in the middle. 'But an honest one!'

Amir's thoughtful pause made her heart jolt uncomfortably as she waited for his reply.

'It was not the answer I hoped I'd hear,' he murmured silkily. 'But you are lucky that I am in an indulgent mood. Shall we go through to the dining room?'

He held out his hand and Lydia had no choice but to put hers into it.

If this was Amir in an *indulgent* mood, she couldn't help thinking, then she really didn't think she wanted to meet him in a less tolerant frame of mind. Just the thought of it made her nerves twist so much that she had to pray her trembling fingers didn't give away her feelings to the man at her side.

CHAPTER FOUR

'HAVE you had enough?'

There was no mistaking the ironical note in Amir's voice, and frankly Lydia was not at all surprised to hear it there.

'I'm—not hungry any more.'

The truth was that she hadn't been hungry from the moment she had sat down at the table. Her appetite had totally deserted her when Amir had slid into the chair directly opposite her, elbows resting on the fine white linen cloth, tanned hands linked, his chin resting on the top of them, deep-set eyes fixed intently on her face.

'Help yourself,' he'd told her softly.

He had watched everything she'd done. That dark gaze had followed each movement of her hands, flicking backwards and forwards as she'd taken a little from each serving dish, spooning it onto her plate, until she'd found herself shivering faintly under that eagle-eyed scrutiny.

'Don't you want anything?' she had managed unevenly as a result of the ragged beating of her heart.

Amir had shaken his dark head.

'Not hungry,' he'd murmured. 'At least, not for food.'

She knew exactly what he meant. It was there in the burn of his brilliant eyes, the undisguised sensuality of that searching gaze. Lydia risked a hasty glance into his stunning face and immediately regretted it as her heart lurched high up into her throat and the hand that held the knife shook betrayingly.

'It—it's very good. This chicken is delicious.'

'Jamila is an excellent cook.'

He couldn't have sounded less interested.

But he didn't rush her. Instead he seemed content to wait and watch as she picked at the food, trying vainly to make some pretence of enthusiasm, struggling to swallow with a throat that had dried in the heat of her response.

In the end she pushed away her plate, unable to cope any longer.

'You've barely eaten a thing.'

'I wasn't as hungry as I thought.'

He must know what he did to her. Must know that that fierce, unblinking gaze was tying her nerves into knots, making her heart race in double-quick time.

'Not even some fruit?'

She looked like a startled deer, Amir reflected inwardly. Not scared exactly, just wary and uncertain. If he made one false move she could be up and gone. But he wasn't going to make that mistake. He wasn't going to rush things. In the airport he had thought that he'd only had minutes to win her over, make his mark on her consciousness; now it seemed that he had all night.

He could wait.

He reckoned she'd be well worth waiting for.

'What about some of this?'

He reached out slowly, took a perfect peach from the large glass bowl. The contrast between the hard strength of his tanned hands and the velvety skin of the fruit was devastatingly sensual. She couldn't drag her gaze away from the long, strong fingers as they curved around the ripe fruit, smoothing it softly.

In just that way would he touch her, she found herself thinking on a shiver. She could imagine how the caress would feel, the strong yet delicate tips of his hands trailing over sensitive nerves, awakening a stinging desire.

He didn't even have to *touch* her! She could feel that reaction already. Her blood sang in her veins, her flesh so sensitised that even the soft brush of her clothes over it was a delicate agony. She knew what was in his mind. They both knew exactly where his thoughts were heading. So why didn't he *say* something? Why didn't he *act*?

'Try it...'

He had sliced off a thin sliver of the fruit and now he held it out to her, leaning forward to hold it level with her mouth so that all she had to do was open her lips. Like a child she did so and Amir dropped the juicy morsel onto her tongue. It was so ripe that it hardly needed to be chewed but slid down her throat so easily.

'Like that?'

His smile did dangerous things to her heart, making it clench on a wave of response, her mouth drying instantly.

'It's—perfect,' she croaked. 'Wonderful.'

'Then have some more.'

This time he kept his hand closer to his own side of the table so that it was Lydia who had to lean towards him in order to receive the fruit. The movement brought her face level with his, meant that she could look nowhere but into the black depths of his eyes. And, having looked, she couldn't turn away but was held transfixed, hypnotised by the golden flare of desire that burned there.

'More?' Amir questioned softly.

'Mmm.'

She couldn't find the strength to answer him but simply nodded. Her mind was too full of the sexual tug of his closeness, drowning in the dark pools of his eyes, to be able to form any words.

There was still a trace of peach juice on her lips and unthinkingly she let her tongue slide out to lick it away. Immediately Amir's dark gaze dropped down to follow the small movement, then flicked back up again, deeper, blacker, more powerful than before.

It was like being bathed in a river of fire. Like sitting directly in the path of the midsummer sun and feeling its heat wash over her. Her blood was aflame, her skin crying out for his touch.

'Amir...' she tried, but he shook his head gently.

'Hush!' he murmured softly, leaning forward once again to rest one forefinger over her lips to silence her. 'There's no need to rush this, darling. We have all the time in the world.'

She wanted only to do as he said. But at the same time she ached to touch him in some way, to know the warmth of his caress, the feel of his skin against hers.

And so she couldn't stop herself from pressing her lips to that restraining finger, taking one, then two, then three soft, lingering kisses with deliberate care. He tasted of peach juice and the intensely personal flavour of his skin, and she thought she had never known anything more wonderful in all her life. And all the time she kept her gaze fixed on his face so that she saw the way he closed his eyes for a moment, the inner struggle he had for control.

'Lydia...'

This time it was Amir who had trouble speaking, the softly accented voice cracking slightly under the effort of control he imposed on it. And because of that she found the strength to smile straight into his eyes.

'I'd like some more, Amir,' she murmured, knowing exactly the effect the deliberate double meaning would have on him. 'Please don't stop now.'

Don't stop! Amir thought hazily. Surely she knew that was the last thing on his mind. His whole body was tight as a bowstring with the tension of wanting her and yet holding back. He ached with it, *hurt* with it, and yet he wouldn't have it any other way.

He could see the effect it was having on her and so, although he could hardly endure the agony of waiting, in the same moment he wanted to prolong it endlessly. To draw out this most delicate of seductions, this tantalising foreplay, until they could both bear it no longer.

'Your wish is my command, my lady.'

He was sure that she barely tasted the next morsel of peach. That she chewed and swallowed on an automatic instinct, unaware of what she was doing. Her eyes were so dark, the pupils dilated until they concealed all but the faintest rim of blue, that she looked as if she had been drugged or stunned by some sort of blow.

'You shall have more—as much as you want.'

There was a tiny trickle of peach juice left at the corner of her mouth, slipping slowly down towards her chin, and automatically he lifted his hand to brush against her skin to wipe it away, then froze. A moment later he had re-placed his finger with the touch of his lips, letting his tongue lick away the faint stickiness and leave it clean.

It was the moment that finally broke his resolve. Having touched her in this way, he found that he was caught, trapped, unable to move away again. Instead he could only linger, turning the gesture into a caress, pressing a slow kiss on the delicate line of her jaw and then another, closer to her mouth.

'Amir...'

It was a choking cry low in her throat, one that told him how close she was to breaking too. And, hearing it, he abandoned all thought of any further restraint, giving in to the wild surge of passion that ripped through his body like a flood tide.

'Lady, you've been asking for this all night!' he mut-tered roughly before a swift, almost violent movement of his head brought their lips together in a hungry kiss.

It was like being thrown straight into the eye of a storm. Thunder crashed in his head, lightning flashing behind his eyes. He couldn't have enough of her lips, couldn't get close enough to her to kiss her properly.

The damn table was right in the way.

With a muttered curse against her mouth, he reached for

her, hauling her towards him, sending cutlery and china scattering, falling to the floor in a series of crashes.

Lydia heard the sounds of the devastation through the roaring haze inside her head. She was aware only of the hard crush of Amir's lips against her own, the grip of powerful hands on her arms, lifting her bodily from her chair and dragging her closer towards him.

She was half on and half off the table, perching awkwardly on the fine cloth, dependent on his strength to keep her from falling. She was blinded by the whirling mist inside her head, unable to see anything of her surroundings, aware only of the fierce intensity of his eyes as they burned down into her.

'Amir...'

Her hands reached for his shoulders, clutching, holding on, initially, for much-needed support. But then her fingers brushed against the warm strip of skin beyond the neckline of the soft cashmere sweater and immediately her touch gentled.

'Amir...' she breathed again, letting her fingers slide over the satin flesh she had longed to touch, for aeons it seemed.

She felt the powerful muscles bunch and clench under her caress, heard his breathing catch in his throat then start up again, raw and uneven, in time with the jagged race of her own heart.

And all the time his mouth plundered hers. First savage, almost cruelly demanding, then gentling, soothing the bruises his inflamed passion had inflicted, and finally tender, so, so tender that her heart melted to liquid inside her and her head swam with the heady delight of it.

'You have bewitched me,' Amir muttered against her cheek. 'Since the moment I first saw you I have been unable to function, unable to *think* of anything beyond this. Beyond the need to kiss you, hold you, touch you...'

His hands were urgent at her waist, tugging her sweater

clear of the band of her jeans. Long fingers pushed up along her ribcage, then down between the denim and her skin as if he couldn't make up his mind what he wanted most to touch. He pulled her even closer, making her slide over the tabletop, sending another plate, another glass hurtling to the floor.

'Amir…' she choked, her protest edged with a tremor of shaky laughter '…we have to stop this.'

'*Never*…' His voice was thick and rough with angry protest, the ferocity of his refusal sending sparks of excited response searing along every nerve.

'No…'

The laughter was more pronounced now, threatening to merge into something close to nervous hysteria.

'I mean, we have to stop this *here*. If we're not careful we're going to wreck the joint. Look…'

Somehow she managed to get her hand between her cheek and his, to turn his face to the side so that he could survey the devastation they had wreaked. For a long moment it seemed that he could not take it in, the jet eyes still glazed with desire, every muscle in his face taut with hunger.

But then, slowly, he blinked and seemed to return to himself, surveying the wreckage with a touch of ruefulness but no real conscience.

'I always hated that dinner service anyway,' he muttered roughly. 'But you're right. This isn't the place for this. We would be far more comfortable upstairs…'

And before Lydia had time to register what was in his mind, he had lifted her bodily from the table, swinging her up into his arms with an ease that revealed the true strength of the muscles underneath the softness of the cashmere. Kicking her chair out of his way, he carried her towards the door.

'Amir!' Lydia protested breathlessly. 'Stop it! You can't…'

But he ignored her, crossing the hall in a few swift strides and turning to mount the first couple of stairs.

The upward movement made Lydia draw in her breath sharply, her arms instinctively going round his neck for security in a way that drew her close against him.

'Amir!' she said again on a very different note.

'What's wrong?' he asked huskily. 'Don't you trust me?'

Trust. The word reverberated inside Lydia's head.

Trust him?

Oh, she trusted him to get her safely up the stairs; she had no doubt about that. She could feel the power in the chest against which her head lay, the iron strength of the arms that held her. She knew that he wouldn't drop her, or fall. Physically, she was quite safe.

But emotionally, it was a very different matter.

Emotionally she had no idea how she was going to come out of this. She couldn't say if she would survive un-scathed, or emerge with just a few faint scars. She had never known anything like it; never known anyone like Amir. And, that being so, she had no way of predicting how she would feel when one day this was over, as it must inevitably be over.

People like her and Amir lived in separate worlds. They didn't usually meet under normal circumstances. If it hadn't been for the chance of fate they would just have been like ships that passed in the night, never making con-tact, never even knowing each other's names.

And wouldn't that have been safer?

'Lydia?'

He'd lost her somewhere, Amir realised. He could feel the wild excitement of just moments before seeping away from them like air from a pricked balloon. If he wasn't careful, it would be gone for good, he told himself, his fiercely aroused body screaming in savage protest at just the thought.

On the half-landing he paused, looking deep into her eyes.

'What is it? Second thoughts?'

'No...' But it didn't sound at all convincing.

'Listen to me...'

Slowly he lowered her to the floor, setting her upright with her back against the wall. Taking her small chin in one strong hand, he tilted her face up so that her hyacinth-blue eyes were forced to meet the black intensity of his gaze.

'Beautiful Lydia, there's no need for doubts. I promise you that I will never harm you. That I will make this the best I can for you. You can trust me with your life.'

When he looked at her like that, she would trust him with her soul. And, oh, she wanted that trust!

She didn't want this distance that had suddenly come between them, wiping away the fizzing, burning excitement of just moments before as if it had just been chalk marks on a blackboard, erased with one wipe of a cloth.

She wanted that excitement back. Wanted it raging through her body like a forest fire, burning in her head, obliterating all doubt, all thought, leaving only feeling. The sort of feeling that broke over her head like a tidal wave, swamping her completely.

And there was a simple, easy way to get it back.

'Kiss me, Amir,' she whispered pleadingly. 'Kiss me and show me how it can be...'

'Willingly...'

It was a rough, harsh mutter as his dark head came down towards hers, his mouth taking her lips with a wild demand.

And in the space of a heartbeat it was as if that moment of hesitation and doubt had never been. The tidal wave of desire swept through her, hot and wild, picking her up and carrying her with it into a world of oblivion. A world where only her body and the fierce, demanding hunger that spiralled deep inside had any relevance at all.

On a cry of delight and surrender, she opened her mouth to him and felt the hot invasion of his tongue. His long, hard frame crushed hers against the wall, heat and steel enclosing her, holding her prisoner. Against the fine bones of her pelvis burned the heated, swollen evidence of his desire for her. Just the feel of it sent a stinging shaft of longing straight into the innermost heart of her femininity so that she moaned aloud in need.

'Yes...'

Amir took the cry into his own mouth and expelled it again as a raw sigh.

'I know exactly how you feel, sweetheart. It gets me that way as well.'

His hands touched her face, her hair, her neck, slid in at the top of her sweater, then down to cover one breast.

'*You* get me that way.'

Lydia moved restlessly against the hard support of the wall, returning each kiss with another, more passionate, less inhibited, her arms closing round his neck, fingers clutching at the black silken strands of his hair.

'I want...I want...'

It was all she could manage but he didn't need any more and his laughter was a dark, sexy sound in her ear.

'Don't worry, darling. I know exactly what you want. For a start, you want this...'

He was edging her along the wall as he spoke, moving her towards the next flight of stairs, the next floor. And as they moved his hands were tugging at the waist of her sweater, pulling it roughly upwards.

Adrift on a hot sea of passion, Lydia made no protest when he wrenched it up and over her head. Instead, she helped him all she could, twisting her arms to free them from the sleeves and tossing the discarded garment aside so that it fell in a crumpled heap on the landing at her feet.

'And you want this…'

Her tee shirt and bra soon followed, dropping onto the step behind her as Amir half walked, half carried her up the next flight of stairs, and she heard her shoes bounce and tumble downwards as she kicked them off impatiently. The sound of the second one thumping all the way to the hall below was the last thing she registered before Amir's hands closed over her exposed breasts and she lost all capability of thought.

His hands burned against her skin, sending blazing shafts of need shooting through her as he cupped and held their soft weight, lifting them gently to meet the caress of his mouth.

'And this…'

Lydia collapsed against the hard wall at her back, grateful for its firm support, for the imprisoning cage of Amir's powerful legs that crushed her thighs. Without them, she felt she would crumple into a boneless heap on the floor, all her strength evaporating in the moment that demanding mouth closed over the tip of one aching breast. Her head went back, her body arching to meet that potent source of pleasure as his tongue swirled sensually over the tightened bud of her nipple, drawing it into the warmth of his mouth.

'Oh, yes, Amir, yes…'

It was an incoherent litany of joy, every ounce of her being concentrated on that one stinging centre of delight. And when his lips closed tightly, to tug and suckle on the sensitive point, she could only give in to the most urgent, primitive part of her, the part that made her clutching fingers twist and tug at his hair, trying to pull him even closer, to prolong and intensify this most thrilling of pleasures.

Somehow they stumbled up the remaining stairs to the landing, and it was only as he lowered her to lie on the wide expanse of soft deep green carpet that Lydia realised that she was almost completely naked. Her jeans and the small sliver of pale blue satin that was her only remaining underwear had been pushed down from her hips, tumbling into a crumpled pool around her ankles so that all she had to do was kick her legs to be free of them.

She didn't have a moment to feel exposed or cold. Barely had the time to blink, certainly not to think about coming out of the haze of hunger that held her in its grip before Amir too had thrown off his clothing and come down on the floor beside her, gloriously naked and forcefully, totally aroused. Just the sight of him made her shudder in nervous excitement.

'But most of all…'

He pulled her towards him, sliding down the soft pile of the carpet, and covered her trembling body with the strength of his.

'What you want is this…'

Capturing both her hands in one of his, he held them pinioned above her head while with his free fingers he subjected her body to the most concentrated sensual assault she had ever known. He stroked every inch of her, found pleasure spots and erotic buttons she hadn't known she possessed. He traced hot trails of excitement over her hypersensitive skin, curved his palm around her breasts, tormented the aching tips with gentle touches and tiny, delicate pinches.

And then, when she thought her mind would explode with the non-stop, endless pleasure that he had given her, he finally took those tormenting caresses all the way down the length of her body, slid them through the damp, warm curls and into the most feminine centre of her body.

'Amir!' Lydia gasped her delight, her body convulsing underneath him.

With a strength that surprised her, she wrenched her hands free, pushing them into his hair. Dragging his head down, she crushed her lips passionately to his, putting all her hunger, all the need that gripped her into the kiss.

'Now,' she muttered against his mouth. 'Oh, please, please, now! Take me *now*!'

The words had barely left her tongue when he thrust into her, wild and hard and so fiercely welcome that her control shattered completely. When he began to move, she went with him, driven by pagan, primitive desires that were more powerful, more irresistible than anything she had ever known.

Each movement of his powerful body brought a new and heightened sensation. Each kiss, each caress took her nearer and nearer to the edge.

'Lydia!' Amir choked, his voice rough and heavy, his eyes blazing with passion, the hot colour streaking his cheeks underlining the ruthless desire that gripped him. 'Lady, you are so *good*. Spectacular! I've never known anyone like you.'

She opened her mouth to tell him that she felt the same but even as she did he drove into her harder than ever before, shattering her thoughts and reducing her to nothing but a raging wildfire, totally beyond management, beyond restraint.

The pulsing inside her head mounted higher and higher, matched by the throbbing, spiralling heat between her legs. She was climbing, soaring, flying, out in the sky, away from the confines of the earth, until at last, with one wild, abandoned cry, she felt herself splinter and the world cascaded around her in a myriad glowing lights.

CHAPTER FIVE

IT WAS something odd about the light, and a quality to the faint sounds of the day that she was unused to, that woke Lydia late the following morning.

For a couple of seconds she lay still, her mind blank and confused, not knowing where she was or how she had got there.

She *should* be in California, she knew. Should be waking up on the first morning of her new life, far away from everything she had wanted to leave behind, ready to start again.

But she wasn't. She was...

Amir!

The name, and with it the realisation, the memories, rushed into her mind with the force of a blow to her head. Her eyes flew open, staring unfocused round her, not knowing whether she was hoping or dreading to see the man who had brought her here.

'So you're awake at last.'

The low husky tones, agonisingly familiar even after so short an acquaintance, brought her head swinging round in shock.

He was sitting in a chair beside the bed, lounging back against the cushions, long legs stretched out on the carpet, arms folded firmly in front of him. He had pulled on jeans but that was all, and the broad, hair-hazed chest was completely naked. His feet were bare, and the lean cheeks, the strong bones of his jaw were shadowed with the dark stubble of a night's growth of beard.

But it was his eyes that drew her the most. Deep and dark and narrowed under heavily hooded lids, they were

fixed on her face, watchful and alert to every faint flicker
of emotion across her sleep-clouded features. And there
was no emotion in them. No warmth. Nothing to give her
any clue to the way he was feeling.

Lydia cleared her throat nervously.

'G-good morning.'

It was all she could think of to say. What *did* one say
to the man who had effectively picked her up at the airport
and brought her here for what was nothing more than a
one-night stand?

One night. But *what* a night!

Hot colour flooded into her cheeks at the memory of the
hours before she had finally fallen into the sleep of total
exhaustion. Her eyes slid away from the steady, searching
stare of the man who had reduced her to that state.

It was too late to feel embarrassed. Too late to scrabble
for the bedclothes and pull them up around her nakedness.
There wasn't an inch of her body that he hadn't seen,
touched, *kissed*, and yet here, in the very cold light of day,
she knew she couldn't face him with any degree of composure unless she was covered from her chin to her toes.

'Good morning.' Amir responded gravely to her shaky
greeting. 'I don't suppose I have to do my duty as your
host and ask whether you slept well.'

'N-no…'

Lydia wished desperately that she could get control of
her voice. The only way to handle this was to be as cool
and collected as he obviously was. To behave as if torrid
one-night stands were very much a part of her life and she
was used to waking up next to men she had known for
barely half a day.

But it was very difficult when the truth was quite the
opposite. She had never had a one-night stand in her life.
And as for 'experience', she doubted that the few, unful-
filling months she had had with Jonathon quite came into
that category.

'I—we—I was worn out.'

The sensual mouth twitched into something that might have been the beginning of a smile, but which was clamped down on hard before it could actually develop.

'We wore each other out,' he acknowledged dryly. 'It was quite a night. One I won't forget in a long, long time.'

'Well, I'm glad that at least I'll prove memorable to you,' Lydia declared, hitching herself up on the pillows and tucking the sheet firmly around her so that it covered her from her breasts downwards. It still didn't conceal the fact that her skin had burned a fiery red at his comment, but it would have to do.

'You'll be more than memorable,' Amir drawled in sardonic reply. 'Unforgettable would be the word I would use.'

'Is that meant to be a compliment?'

His tone had made the description decidedly ambiguous. So she didn't know whether to trust the quick, sharp flare of delight at the thought that this devastating man would find her impossible to erase from his memory.

'You can take it whatever way you like.'

Right now, he wasn't exactly sure how he meant it himself. The events of the previous night had knocked him for six from the start and he had been trying to catch up with his feelings ever since.

He only knew that most of the time he hadn't been thinking with his mind—certainly not with his intelligence—but with a far more basic part of his make-up.

But one thing was certain. He would never, *ever* forget the experience he had had last night, though the truth was that most of the details were decidedly hazy. From the moment that he had kissed away the trickle of peach juice from the corner of her mouth he had been caught up in a sexual firestorm that had taken possession of him right to his very soul and he had been incapable of thinking as a result.

He had simply *felt*. By Allah, how he had felt! He had never known such a concentrated, non-stop, mind-blowing tornado of pleasure as the one that had had him in its grip. Even now, just to think of it made his body harden in pleasurable recollection combined with an aching demand, so intense it was close to pain, that he repeat the experience all over again. And seeing Lydia sitting there in the bed—in *his* bed—with the sheet pulled up so closely round her was doing nothing to help his self-control.

'Would you like a tee shirt or something?' he demanded abruptly, seeing her blink in stunned confusion. 'To wear, I mean,' he elucidated when she frowned her bewilderment.

'I'm quite warm enough, thank you.'

'It wasn't your warmth or the lack of it I was thinking of. I meant that perhaps we would both be better able to concentrate if you had some clothes on.'

She thought she was removing all temptation, he knew. She believed she was acting prim and proper, concealing the parts of her that were likely to inflame lustful thoughts and so reducing the possibility of him being distracted by the sight of her body. She couldn't be more wrong.

Didn't she know that the soft linen sheet clung to every curve of her body? That it undulated over the soft mounds of her breasts, flowed down over the flat stomach and long, slim legs? Wasn't she aware of the way that, because the material was so fine, he could see the faint dark shadow between her legs? With the memory of how it had felt to bury himself in those curls still so strong in his mind, it was all he could do not to lurch out of this chair, fling back the covers to expose her tantalising nakedness and make love to her all over again.

At least they would have the comfort of a bed this time. Last night it had taken them a long time to even reach the bedroom, never mind the bed itself. It was only after the first fire of hunger had ebbed a little, after they had appeased their urgent, aching need for each other, that he had been able even to think of carrying her in here and placing her on the bed.

And just that brief respite had been enough to stoke the embers once again. The feel of her slim, soft body in his arms had been more than he'd been able to bear. He had no sooner lowered her onto the mattress than he had had to have her again. And she had responded every bit as hungrily to him.

No! Enough was enough! He couldn't think straight. He couldn't *think* at all.

Pushing himself out of the chair, he strode across to the cupboards, yanked open a drawer and snatched up the nearest tee shirt.

'Here!'

He almost flung it in her direction, refusing to let himself look while she struggled into the soft blue cotton without letting the sheet slip any lower.

'What do we have to concentrate on?' she asked, her voice still muffled by the enfolding garment.

'We have to talk.'

Amir couldn't bring himself to go back and sit down again. He found it much easier to give in to the restlessness he was feeling by pacing about the room, moving across the floor from one window to the other.

'Talk about what?'

Oh, Lydia, don't be a *fool*! Don't you know? Can't you guess? A one-night stand was all it was. He'd had his fun—he'd got what he wanted and now he wanted out.

'About us.'

'There is no—'

'I've been in touch with the airport.'

'Oh-h-h.'

It was a faint sigh. A sound of despondency that she couldn't hold back. Of course he'd been in touch with the airport. He wanted out—he wanted rid of her and he'd been determined to find out just how quickly it could be managed. What else had she expected?

'I rang them first thing.'

Naturally. She wished he would stand still, stop this restive pacing. He reminded her far too much of a hungry panther, prowling impatiently about its territory, looking for its next prey.

Well, she could make it easy for him.

'When does my flight leave? Luckily I don't have anything to get ready, because I never even unpacked. All I have to do is get my clothes…'

Her voice trailed off as she realised just what that would entail. She would have to go on a hunt for all the clothing she had discarded in stages on the way upstairs last night. Her shoes would probably have fallen into the hall. Her jumper would be on the half-landing, her bra beside it. And as for her jeans and panties…

'Here…'

Amir had picked something up from a chair and now he dumped the bundle on the end of the bed. Seeing what it was, Lydia coloured sharply, wishing the floor would open up and swallow her whole before she died of embarrassment and regret.

Her clothes. He had collected up all her clothes, even the shoes, folded them neatly and had them ready for her to put on. Was he so anxious for her to be gone?

'Thank you.' She forced herself to say it. 'I can be washed and dressed and out of your hair in five minutes flat. If you'll just…'

'No.'

It was flat and emotionless, bringing her head up in a shocked rush. His eyes were as unrevealing as his tone, impossible to read.

'No? No, what? No, I can't get dressed—or you don't believe I can get dressed in five minutes? No, you don't want me to use your bathroom?'

'I have no doubt that if you wanted to you could get dressed in much less than five minutes—much as I would prefer it if you didn't. But what I actually meant was, no, you can't leave.'

It was that 'can't' that did it. Thrown at her like a regal decree from the Crown Prince he was, it made her blood run cold, shivers slithering down her spine.

'And you can't make me stay!' she protested, sitting up sharply in bed. 'You're not in Kuimar now, *Highness*! You can't hold me against my will! There are laws against this sort of thing.'

At last Amir had stilled his restless movement. Standing between her and the door, he regarded her thoughtfully, with a definite wicked gleam in his dark eyes.

'I have no intention of holding you against your will, my dear Ms Ashton. And you won't need to invoke British or indeed international law against me. For one thing, I doubt if it would have any effect on the weather.'

'The weather?'

Lydia frowned her bewilderment.

'What has the weather got to do with this?'

'Everything. As I said, I phoned the airport first thing. The snow has been coming down all night, and fog has made matters even worse. They don't think they'll get the runways clear for three days at the least.'

'Is this the truth?'

Lydia eyed him suspiciously, frank disbelief shadowing her eyes.

'You wouldn't lie to me about it?'

'What benefit would there be for me in lying?' The look he turned on her was totally guileless—on the surface at least. 'What would it do for me?'

Why didn't he just say, I wouldn't go to the trouble of lying to keep *you* here? Lydia wondered grumpily, her mood aggravated by the unexpected pain in her heart at the thought.

'So I can't get away? There are no planes at all?'

'Not for three days—more if conditions worsen.'

'But what am I going to do?'

Now it was Lydia's turn to want to pace uneasily about the room. She made a move to fling back the covers and get out of bed in a way that expressed the unease and disturbance in her mind. But then, recalling the fact that the tee shirt she was wearing, although roomy enough, barely came down to the tops of her thighs, she hastily rethought. Instead she perched on the edge of the bed, with the sheets pulled over her legs.

'What about my job? Where can I stay?'

'There's plenty of room here.'

It was the last thing she had expected. Having convinced herself that he was anxious for her to leave, that he couldn't wait to see the back of her, she had never thought to hear him offer her any sort of help, let alone accommodation.

'You'd let me stay?'

'I'd like it,' he declared, shocking her even further with the note of sincerity that rang in his voice. 'Look, Lydia…'

He came back to the chair he had been sitting in, settled on the arm of it so that he was exactly level with her and could look her straight in the eyes, intent jet gaze meeting wary blue.

'I've already told you that last night was something I won't forget in a long time. It's also something I'd like to repeat—given the chance.'

He paused briefly, but just as Lydia was wondering whether she was supposed to be saying 'me, too', and speculating whether it would be wise or far too revealing, he went on in a more sombre tone.

'But right now…'

'Oh, I should have known there was bound to be a "but"!'

Lydia was shocked by her own outburst, and the bitterness of the tone she used. She hadn't been prepared for the way that 'But right now…' had torn at her heart. And the realisation of exactly why that had hurt so much rocked her sense of reality dangerously.

How could she have let this man sneak into her heart after knowing him for such a short time? It wasn't even twenty-four hours since they had met! She knew almost nothing about him beyond his name and the fact that he was a wonderful lover. That was hardly a basis for coming to care about anyone!

'Well, it's all right, you don't have to spell it out. I can get the message as well as anyone. I'll even say it for you, shall I? It was great—I'll see you around. Thanks for everything. Or perhaps you were planning on adding, I'll give you a ring some time—like I'd be fool enough to believe that!'

The cool scrutiny of those deep eyes was disturbing, making her shift nervously on the bed, wondering just what was going on in that calculating mind.

'Don't you think you're rather rushing to conclusions?' he enquired softly, unsettling her even more.

'What other conclusion is there to come to? I'm not a child, Amir. Nor am I a silly schoolgirl brought up on comic-strip stories of love at first sight and happily ever after. I know that having sex—even the fantastic, mind-blowing sort of sex we shared—isn't any sort of guarantee of a deeper feeling. In fact it's usually not. It was probably the fact that we're complete strangers that made it that way.'

'But you agree that it was fantastic?' Amir inserted smoothly when she paused for breath.

Too late to back out now. She'd already opened her big mouth way too wide on that score.

'Well, yes.'

She tried desperately to sound offhand, as if thrilling,

mind-blowing sex with total strangers was something she experienced almost every second day.

'And that being so, it's something you'd like to repeat?'

'Might do. I don't know…'

What was she getting herself into here?

'Well, I do. I know I'd like to repeat the experience over and over again. But there's a problem.'

Of course. Now they were coming to it.

'For certain reasons—commitments I can't get out of—my life's not my own right now. I'm not a free agent. I certainly wasn't planning on starting any relationship with anyone, and, if that plane had left on time yesterday, I wouldn't be doing so now.'

He paused as if expecting some comment, but Lydia couldn't think of one to make. Added to that, her tongue seemed to have frozen in her mouth, and she couldn't have forced it to form a single word if she'd tried.

'But then, of course, I met you.'

And meeting Lydia had scrambled his thought patterns, driven all common sense from his head. For the space of a few crazy, heated hours last night he had forgotten all about his father and the conditions the stiff-necked old man had placed on his future. He'd forgotten all he'd fought for over the past years, the ambition that had driven him since his eleventh birthday.

But this morning a degree of sanity had returned. He wasn't going to throw over all he'd worked for. For years he'd got nowhere, feeling as if he were beating his head hard against a brick wall. Then, just as he had come close to deciding that it was time to give up, that the arrogant, cold-hearted old bastard just wasn't worth the effort, suddenly Sheikh Khalid had held out an olive branch. But an olive branch that had come with a price tag attached.

It was a price tag he could cope with. The end result would be well worth the small sacrifice he'd have to make. But that price tag meant that dalliance with other women, even women as appealing and enticing as Miss Lydia Ashton, was out.

And so he'd resolved that, no matter how much he might regret it, he had to make sure she was on the first plane out of London for California, heading for that dream job of hers and out of his life. Which was why he'd got onto the airport first thing.

Only to find that there would be no flights to anywhere for the foreseeable future.

'Another day, another time, it might have been different. We could have had some fun together for a while. But I don't have that while.'

'I see.'

Lydia's voice was flat, dreary, monotone. For a few wonderful moments there she had actually allowed herself to dream, to hope. To let a tiny chink of expectation slide into her mind and start to take root.

The hope that Amir might want more than the one-night stand.

Stupid! Foolish! Downright *naïve*!

Men like Amir didn't fall for women like her. They didn't lose their hearts to ordinary, everyday girls from ordinary, everyday families in ordinary, everyday towns.

Amir was a *sheikh*, for heaven's sake! A *Crown Prince*! He moved in elevated circles filled with wealthy, sophisticated women. Women who could embark on a casual affair without so much as a second thought and leave it again when the time came, without bothering to glance back.

Meeting her in the VIP lounge at the airport, he must have assumed that she belonged there. That she was as classy and urbane as the women he was used to mixing with. He'd had no way of knowing that the only thing that was classy about her was the job she had been heading off to.

'Well, it's all right, I'm not going to be difficult. I know a brush-off when I get one…'

'Dammit, Lydia, no!'

Once more Amir got to his feet in a swift fluid movement that expressed perfectly his impatience, the annoyance that sparked deep in his dark eyes.

'You're not listening to me! I'm not giving you the brush-off!'

'You're not?'

Try as she might, she couldn't stop her mouth from trembling in shock so that the words came out on a revealing quaver.

'Then what—?' she tried again but Amir cut across her swiftly.

'At least, not right now.'

Drawing in his breath on a sharp, resolute hiss, he raked both strong hands through the sleek gleaming silk of his hair before he fixed his eyes on her perturbed face once more.

'What I'm trying to say is that I can't offer anything with a future, anything more than a passing affair—and a brief one at that. Yesterday I thought we couldn't have more than that night, but this morning I discovered that fate has dealt us a very different hand of cards to the ones we originally had. The airports are closed; we can't go anywhere. We have an unexpected three days, Lydia. Three days we can spend together, if you want to.'

'If I…'

She couldn't finish the sentence, a rush of panicky self-preservation warring with the instinctive, yearning hunger in her mind. Her thoughts swung this way and that, whirling frantically, unable to come up with anything close to a decision.

Amir had taken her hands in his, enclosing her fingers and gripping them tight. His eyes burned as they held hers, willing her to do as he wanted.

'I can offer you three days, and the nights that go with them, Lydia. Nothing more. Three days together and then we go our separate ways. What do you say? Is it yes or no?'

CHAPTER SIX

THREE days!

He was offering her three days. Nothing more.

Three days. And the nights that went with them. Don't forget those nights.

How *could* she forget the nights?

Three days, three nights. It was nothing. It was everything.

When she'd been thinking this would only ever be a one-night stand, it was all she'd ever dreamed of. And it was so much less than she had truly dreamed of.

'Lydia?'

Amir gave her hand a little shake to bring her back to the present.

'What do you say?'

What *could* she say? Every sense of self-preservation warned her not even to consider it. All that was the old Lydia, calm, rational, cautious, declared loudly that she would be selling herself short, that there was no future in what he offered. At the end of the three days he would leave her, hurt and used, and go his own selfish way.

'Three days…'

'I know it isn't long, but it's all I have. All we have. It's that or nothing.'

'You certainly give it to me straight.'

Lydia hoped that her smile worked, that it hid the confusion and the hurt in her eyes.

'There's no other way to give it. I'm not offering any more, Lydia. There isn't anything more. But in those three days—and especially in the three nights we share—I promise you we'll have the affair of a lifetime.'

70

'Sounds tempting.'

Her words snapped off on a hasty intake of breath as he slid an arm around her waist and gently drew her close. Bending his head, he touched his lips to the soft fall of her hair then came even closer and laid his cheek against hers. The intensely personal scent of his skin filled her nostrils and the faint shadow of stubble rasped over her tender flesh.

'Then let me tempt you, sweetheart,' he murmured against her ear. 'Let me persuade you to stay and I promise you you'll never forget it. You can have anything you want. Everything you want.'

Everything except his love.

No!

Where had that crazy thought come from? She hadn't been considering the prospect of *love*. Love was something she had no place for in her life right now. It was the last thing she wanted. It would complicate things far too much.

'Everything?'

'Anything,' he confirmed deeply, his mouth moving gently against her skin, pressing on it slow, delicate kisses that stirred her senses to the depths of her soul. 'You only have to ask.'

Those kisses were stopping her from thinking. They were waking the deepest, most primitive longings in her. Hunger uncoiled between her legs, burning along her nerves like a forest fire. She couldn't stay passive any more and, with a swift twist of her neck, she turned her head so that her mouth was under his and she kissed him, hard and fierce.

For a second even Amir seemed taken aback. He stilled suddenly, dark head going back just an inch or two so that those ebony eyes could look straight into her wide blue ones.

'Lydia?' he questioned softly.

At the mercy of the clamouring demand of her body,

she had no time for hesitation, or fear. She met the searching demand of that concentrated stare head-on, not even
blinking in its power.

Taking his head in her hands, slender fingers lying along
the lean planes of his cheeks, shaping the hard bones, she
drew him closer, took his mouth in another kiss, slower
and more lingering this time.

'Lydia…' he said again, but in a very different tone.
'What is this?'

The faint unevenness of the question emboldened her,
gave her a new and intoxicating sense of power. Her smile
straight into those watchful eyes was confident, gleaming
with female triumph, holding a distinct edge of provoca-
tive challenge.

'You said I only had to ask.'

For the space of a single heartbeat he closed his eyes.
And when he opened them again the coal-dark depths were
lit from within by the golden flare of desire.

'And you're asking?'

Lydia nodded slowly, still holding his gaze with her
own.

'For everything?'

She nodded again, her mouth drying in the heat of her
need.

'For everything,' she croaked. 'And anything…'

'Then you'll have everything,' he told her huskily. 'Everything I can give you and more.'

His mouth took hers again as his arms came around her,
sliding under her legs, lifting her from the floor. He carried
her to the bed, laid her down, still with his lips plundering
hers, the erotic dance of his tongue making her senses
swim.

The skimpy tee shirt was no barrier to his urgent hands;
his jeans almost as easily dispensed with. His touch was
on her skin, her face, her breasts. And as she held out her
arms and welcomed him into her body once more Lydia

knew that she had made her decision and she had no intention of going back on it.

Three days. She had three days, and she was going to make the best of them.

When she had thought she would only have one night to remember, then three days seemed like a lifetime in comparison. Three days and three nights stretched ahead, seemingly endless, swollen with possibilities, an eternity of happiness.

Ruthlessly she squashed down the protests, the concerns of the other, the more cautious Lydia. She had been planning on a whole new beginning anyway. She had dreamed of breaking free of the constraints and the prudence that Jonathon had so scorned. The old Lydia might have feared the consequences. The new one embraced the experience willingly, opening her mind and her heart to it.

'I want everything!' she muttered against the heat of Amir's skin, matching her words to the rhythm of his powerfully thrusting body. 'I want everything—everything.'

'And you'll get it,' he promised thickly. 'Believe me, darling, you can have anything you want.'

Anything. Anything. It was like a litany of belief in her head, throbbing, pounding, rising to a crescendo in the moment that her control shattered and she cried out, clinging hard to his powerful shoulders, abandoning herself totally to him.

Anything.

Everything.

For three days.

But even the final reminder of reality that slid into her consciousness as her pulse finally slowed, her breathing eased, and she found herself able to think again had no effect on her decision.

So what if, after the three days, Amir left her without a second thought? What if he walked away and never looked back? Jonathon had done exactly that, and she had been so careful with Jonathon. She had taken things slowly, waited and held back before committing herself. And he had still walked out on her life, discarding her for someone else.

At least Amir had made no pretence of a future. He had been totally straight and upfront from the first. What she saw was what she got. And she was going to embrace that wholeheartedly, no holding back. Taking everything there was on offer.

Beside her Amir stirred lazily, drawing in a deep, contented sigh as he stretched like an indolent cat before a fire.

'Okay?' he asked, his breathing faintly uneven.

'Mmm.'

It was all Lydia could manage. Her heart was still pounding, as much from the significance of her decision as from the explosion of pleasure that had crashed through her.

A long, tanned arm snaked round her waist, whipcord strong muscles tautening to hold her tight as he came up on one elbow to kiss her arm, her cheek, her temple, and look down into her passion-sated face.

'You're sure?' he questioned softly. 'No regrets?'

Lifting her head, Lydia brushed her lips against his cheek, kissed his mouth, then dropped back on the pillow again.

'No,' she assured him confidently, her conviction blazing in her eyes. 'No regrets, none at all.'

'There's just one problem,' Lydia said an hour or so later when, having made love once again, they were finally forced by sheer hunger to think of leaving the bedroom at last. 'Something we hadn't thought of.'

'Oh?'

Amir had just come out of the shower in the *en suite* bathroom and was padding across the carpet, totally unselfconscious in his nudity, to pull open a couple of drawers and extract clothes from inside them.

'And what's that? Nothing important, I hope.'

'Could be quite important,' Lydia informed him, lounging back against the pillows in blissful laziness, her whole body limp and glowing from his attentions.

'What is it?'

Amir paused in his selection of clothing and swung round to face her.

He really had the most wonderful body, Lydia thought dreamily. Perfect. Tall and strong. Lean and muscular, without an ounce of excess weight anywhere on his powerful frame. The wide, strong wall of his chest was softly shaded with black silky hair that arrowed down to a narrow waist and hips and the long, long legs were as well built as the rest of him. And every glorious inch was covered in that smooth, tanned skin that made her fingers itch to touch it again, her mouth hunger to kiss it all over.

'What? *Lydia!*'

The sharpness of Amir's tone startled her out of her wanton daydream, forcing her to turn startled eyes on his exasperated face.

'Oh—sorry—what?'

'I said what is it? What's this problem you've just thought of?'

'It's nothing much…'

'Tell me.'

'Oh, all right. I suppose it might matter after all. I mean we do have to— Sorry!'

She broke off hastily as he gave a small growl of annoyance, rolling his eyes in a gesture of impatience.

'Sorry!' she said again. 'It's just that I don't happen to have any clothes. At least, nothing other than the ones I stood up in yesterday. If you remember, all my luggage was already checked in before the flight was cancelled and we—I—I never thought to go back and collect it before we came here.'

He hadn't thought of it either, Amir admitted privately. He hadn't thought of very much at all. If the truth were told, he hadn't been thinking at all, just acting purely on the sexual hunger that had overwhelmed them from the start and driven them blindly so that last night had been the only natural, inevitable conclusion of their meeting. Last night and the passion they had shared again this morning. A force as old as time, as primitive and powerful as life itself. Something too strong to be denied; too compelling to resist.

'So you see, I don't have anything to wear. Not if I'm going to stay here for three days and three...'

'And three nights,' Amir finished for her as the sentence faded away and hot colour washed over her whole body. 'Not that you have anything to worry about there. What you have on—or, rather, what you don't have on at this moment will be perfect for then.'

Lydia squirmed uncomfortably against the downy pillows, all her earlier ease evaporating like mist before the sun as he subjected her to a slow, lingeringly insolent survey from those burning dark eyes. She was suddenly a prey to a desperate need to snatch at the sheets and pull them up to cover her hastily, concealing every inch of her exposed body from him.

But she struggled to resist it. She could just imagine what Amir's response might be, the mocking gleam that would light in his eyes, the sardonic note that would colour his voice when he commented satirically that it was far, far too late for such thoughts of modesty now.

And he would be right. But that didn't change how she felt. She didn't know what was suddenly different; why she no longer felt totally comfortable in her nakedness when she had been so happy, so confident only moments before. But it was as if a chill wind had suddenly got up, feathering cold breezes over her exposed flesh and making her shiver.

'And as far as I'm concerned, you can stay like that for the whole three days,' Amir continued, pulling on his own clothes as he spoke. The gleam in his eyes had brightened, his appreciative smile turning into a wicked, sexy grin. 'I'd certainly have no objection to you wandering around the apartment stark naked...'

'Well I would!' Lydia snapped sharply, something in his tone making her skin prickle in unease. 'You're not going to play the sheikh with me, *Your Highness*.'

The barb hit home with more force than she had dreamed. She saw his long back stiffen, brilliant jet black eyes narrowing swiftly.

'And what,' he ground out harshly, 'is that supposed to mean?'

There was danger in his tone, a warning to be very careful, but Lydia determined to ignore it. He might be Crown Prince in his own country but he was only a man here in the privacy of his bedroom.

'Oh, you know—it smacks too much of the harem. Of the sheikh's favourite being brought out of purdah to be paraded in front of her master, dressed only in the seven veils...'

But she'd gone too far; his expression told her that. The stunning features had set into hard, cold lines, and the sensual mouth was no longer smiling, but clamped tight shut as if to hold back the rush of furious words he could barely keep in check.

'That is *not* what I meant!' he declared coldly. 'And you damn well know it.'

'Oh, do I?'

She no longer cared if he commented on her sudden modesty. She just knew she could no longer face him unless she covered herself and fast.

Snatching up the sheet, she coiled it round her, pulling

it tight into a sort of makeshift toga and tucking the ends in firmly. At least covered in some sort of way, she felt better able to face that angry gaze.

'It seems to me that it's exactly what you meant! That you wanted me here only for your pleasure and you weren't thinking of me... Are you *laughing*?'

He was too. And the worst thing was that all she could think of was the way that amusement warmed those stunning eyes. The smile on the beautiful mouth was wide and unrestrained, showing white, strong teeth. Aloof and distant and in pure Crown Prince mode, he had a masculine beauty that tore at her heart, but like this, easy and relaxed and oh, so human, he would be far too tempting to fall in love with.

No! Not that word again! Hastily she blanked it out, slamming the door shut in her mind.

She had to keep *love* out of this! There was no place for it in a three-day affair with no future.

'Lydia, *habibti*.' Infuriatingly, Amir was still smiling. 'If you'll get off your high horse, you'll see that you're wasting precious time. We only have three days, remember. We don't have time for arguments. And if you're truly worried about the clothes, then don't. We'll soon sort that out.'

'We will?'

She was still not sure she was ready to be appeased. Irritation prickled down her spine, and she had to bite back a hasty retort.

'How will we do that?'

'Leave it to me.'

He shrugged on a black long-sleeved polo shirt, tucking the base of it into the waist of his jeans and swiftly buckling the broad leather belt.

'But I'll make us something to eat first. I'm starving, and I'm sure you must feel the same.'

'I am hungry,' honesty forced Lydia to admit, struggling

against the feeling that she was being deliberately distracted, her thoughts diverted into other paths.

'Then have a shower and come downstairs. You'll have to wear your old clothes for now, but after breakfast we'll go shopping.'

'Shopping?'

Yes, that was guaranteed to soothe whatever had ruffled her feathers, Amir told himself cynically. The effect was instant, her head going back, eyes brightening. It was a trick that never failed. One hundred per cent success rate every time. Once a woman knew who he was—who his father was—it was only a matter of time before she started to work out just what his wealth could buy her.

He had to admit that this Lydia had lasted longer than most. Cleverly, she'd waited for him to come up with the idea, instead of suggesting it herself. But the end result was always the same. He was going to have to pay for the pleasure of her company in his bed.

'Can we go out in all this snow?'

'No problem. The airport may be closed because of ice and fog, but we can still get around town. At least we can go as far as necessary to buy you what you need.'

Lydia blinked in stunned confusion.

'You're going to *buy* me clothes?'

'I knew that would get your interest.'

On his way out the door, Amir had clearly not heard her properly and as a result he had interpreted her reaction as one of stunned delight, instead of which she was simply stunned—and not quite sure how she felt about this development.

'I never knew a woman yet who could resist the thought of going shopping for something new to wear. Yes, I'll buy you the clothes. But only if you hurry up and get dressed so that we can eat before I fade away completely.'

He was gone, running down the stairs, whistling softly, before Lydia could think of a suitable retort.

She was in the shower, washing her hair under the hot running water when realisation dawned. *Now* she knew why that change of mood had come over her. She knew exactly what had caused it. It was happening again now, just to think of it, the heat of the shower barely reaching her as she suddenly felt chilled to the bone.

'As far as I'm concerned, you can stay like that for the whole three days...'

Could he have spelled it out any more clearly?

She had been right to crush back those foolish, naïve thoughts that had kept sliding into her mind. Why had she ever even let herself allow the word 'love' to form at all? It was obvious that Amir had no such thing in his mind. Instead, he had made it plain that he saw her as only one thing—as a sex object, nothing more.

Lydia shivered as she forced herself to face facts. Could she really go through with this? Could she really accept the little he had to offer and not look for more, even for just three days? It was so alien to her way of thinking, her way of feeling, that wouldn't it destroy her?

But then she remembered the feel of Amir's hands on her body, the caress of his lips, the taste of his kisses, and the chill vanished, driven back by a flood of hungry, demanding heat. The heavy pounding of the water down onto her head was echoed in the pulse of need in her body.

If she closed her eyes she could relive those wild, passionate moments in Amir's arms, the sensual onslaught of his lovemaking, the blazing crescendo that had been her orgasm. She wanted *that* again—and again. Wouldn't she sacrifice feeling, emotion, sentiment for it, for the short time it was offered to her?

Yes, of course she would. But that didn't mean she had to sell herself short. Fired by a new determination, she switched off the shower and stepped out of the stall, reaching for a towel and rubbing herself briskly all over. She would show Amir that there was more to this affair than simply sex, she resolved. But he might take some careful handling while she did it.

CHAPTER SEVEN

'YOU took your time.'

Amir greeted Lydia casually when she finally appeared in the doorway of the huge, ultra-modern kitchen.

'The coffee's been ready for ages. So much for your boast that you could be dressed and ready in five minutes flat.'

'That was when I thought I was out of here for good.' Lydia hid the nervous thud of her heart behind a pretence of airy indifference. 'There wouldn't have been much point doing my hair or anything then.'

'But with the prospect of a little retail therapy on the cards, you thought you'd make the effort. The cards in question being my credit cards, of course.'

The cynicism in his tone made Lydia flinch, the resolve that had buoyed her up on her way downstairs receding fast, leaving her feeling limp and flat and desperately uncertain.

'You offered!' she protested.

'So I did. And don't worry, darling, I'll deliver—but after breakfast. I'll die if I don't have a coffee soon. Do you want to eat in here or—'

'Here,' Lydia broke in hastily.

She had peeped into the dining room on her way to the kitchen and had been subject to distinctly ambiguous feelings at the realisation that the chaos they had left behind on the previous night had been carefully tidied away. The remains of the meal had been removed, the disordered tablecloth, the damaged china swept up, presumably by Jamila or someone like her.

'It's warmer in here—more—friendly.'

82

She had been about to say 'more intimate' but had a hasty rethink. 'Intimate' was not a word she was comfortable with when used in the context of Amir.

The short journey downstairs from the bedroom to the kitchen had been a decidedly unsettling one. The realisation that she barely knew where any room in this house was, except for the bedroom, had brought home to her with shocking force just how little she knew about the man she had just spent the night with. The man she had been *intimate* with and with whom she had promised to spend every minute of the next three days.

Amir was a man who routinely flew first class, whose father owned this huge apartment, who had servants who appeared, silently and without needing any instruction, it seemed, to clear away any mess he might make.

What was she doing in the life of someone like that?

'So, what sort of clothes would you like?' Amir asked when, with the coffee poured, she had settled at the long wooden table with a plate of fluffy scrambled eggs and toast. 'What exactly did you have in mind?'

'I've been thinking about that…'

To her annoyance, Lydia found that her throat had suddenly dried, making her voice crack embarrassingly, and she reached for her coffee and drank some hastily to ease her discomfort.

'I'm not happy with the thought of you buying me anything. I mean, I won't need very much anyway—just something to change into—some clean underwear… Why are you looking at me like that?'

Amir lifted broad shoulders in a casual shrug.

'Because if you mean what you say, then I don't believe that you're actually real.'

'Why? Just because I don't want you to spend your money on me?'

'I can afford it.'

'I'm sure you can, but that doesn't mean I like the idea. That isn't what I want from you.'

'It isn't?'

In his experience, it was *exactly* what was wanted.

'Then what *do* you want?'

'I…'

How did she answer that? Stupid, impossible words like 'love' and 'commitment' and 'a future' rushed into her thoughts and she had to drive them away hastily, suddenly fearful that if she let them in, allowed them to take root in her mind, she might actually believe them.

'I don't know. I—I don't usually do this sort of thing. I…'

Suddenly inspiration struck and she seized on it thankfully, jumping to her feet in a rush.

'I know—wait a minute… Where did I leave my bag?'

When she came back into the kitchen a few moments later, clutching her hand luggage, Amir stared at her in frank bemusement as she scrabbled about in the flight bag, hunting for something.

'Lydia…'

'It's in here somewhere. Oh, yes!'

On an exclamation of triumph she pulled out a glossy magazine and dropped it onto the table.

'I don't usually buy this, but I wanted something to read on the plane and this…this caught my eye.'

She wasn't going to admit that she had also bought it because it was so totally unlike anything she normally read. That, filled with the spirit of adventure, the thought of a new start in life, she had picked this just because it was so different. That until now its mixture of celebrity gossip and articles on sex had never appealed in the slightest.

Amir regarded the brightly coloured cover, with its close-up photograph of a pouting, scantily clad model with an expression that was a blend of contempt and disbelief stamped onto his aristocratic features.

'And what, precisely, am I supposed to be looking at?'

'There's an article in here...'

Lydia forced herself to ignore the edge of amusement in his voice as she flicked through the pages hurriedly.

'I know, I was looking at it just before... There!'

She realised her mistake as soon as she had pushed the magazine across the table towards him. She couldn't have given herself away any more clearly if she had made up a placard that said, 'Totally unsophisticated. Never had an affair in her life,' and hung it round her neck.

As she watched Amir smooth down the pages of the magazine with long, elegant fingers she felt what little was left of her confidence seep out of her, leaving her feeling limp and completely stupid. He studied the article as if it were something strange and exotic that he'd never encountered before, a faint frown creasing the space between his black, arched brows.

'"The sensual stages of a super-sexy affair. From first kiss to yes, I do, or no, I don't,"' he drawled sardonically, lifting sceptical eyes to her pink-cheeked face. 'My dear Lydia, what *is* this?'

And have you gone completely out of your mind? He didn't actually put the question into words but it was there in his expression, in the tone of his voice.

'Are you suggesting that it's some sort of blueprint for our relationship?'

That carefully controlled patience in his words did more to express his mood than any less tolerant demand, and it set Lydia's heart fluttering in her throat.

'Well, yes—it could be that,' she improvised hastily. 'We have just three days together, and we want to make the most of it—yes?'

He was still regarding her as if he thought she had had some sort of dangerous brainstorm, but when she glanced at him questioningly he inclined his dark head in brusque agreement.

'Good, I thought you weren't with me then. We don't want to miss out any part of what makes—'

'A super-sexy affair…' Amir inserted ironically, almost destroying her ability to go on.

'I wouldn't put it quite that way myself.'

Jonathon would recognise that voice. Prim and proper, lips pulled tight like a purse-string, was what he had once called it. Remembering that she was supposed to be a very different person from the one Jonathon had known, Lydia made a determined effort to relax.

'But I did think it would be fun to try and fit in all these stages into the three days. Don't you agree?'

Pulling out a chair, she sat back down at the table and turned the magazine round so that she could read it properly. Concentrating hard on the text made it easier to forget that Amir was watching her, powerful black eyes fixed intently on her downbent head.

'Obviously we'll have to cram them up a bit. We can't wait—what's this one? Six months or so before we go on holiday together—we can hardly do that. But if we adapt and adjust here and there, I'm sure we could do them all— or come close to it. What do you think?'

'If that's what you'd like…'

He had to admit that she constantly surprised him, this Lydia Ashton. He never quite knew just what sort of a woman she would be next. From the moment she had frozen him out at their first meeting, to the wild, wanton creature she had been in his bed, she had had a dozen different faces and personalities, all of them intriguing and appealing in their own way.

And now she was someone else again. Suddenly the careful control of earlier that morning had slipped away, to be replaced with a youthful enthusiasm that was almost childlike in its bubbling excitement.

It was the distant opposite of the sort of sophisticated boredom and indifference he was accustomed to in many of the women he knew and in spite of himself he found it unexpectedly appealing. He also wanted it to continue, to keep Lydia with him for longer. And if playing along with her crazy idea of following this list did that, then he was prepared to do so.

'I'm sure we can manage something.'

'You'll go along with it? Great!'

She was painfully aware of the way that she was using enthusiasm to hide her inner insecurity.

'We don't have to do them in exactly this order, of course. For a start there are a couple of things we can cross off already.'

Pulling a pen from her handbag, she ticked off the first item on the list in the magazine.

'Meeting, for one, obviously. And first kiss…'

'And some of them we've rather jumped the gun on,' Amir put in dryly.

One long finger tapped an entry lower down the page, a devilish glint lighting his eyes as they looked up and into hers.

Seeing that the paragraph he had pointed to read, 'After a month to six weeks—you go to bed together', she coloured fierily.

'Yes, well, that's the way it's meant to be—we only have seventy-two hours, so we can't hang about.'

'And you can cross this one off too.'

Another gesture of his hand indicated the section on 'moving in together'.

'All right!' Lydia knew when she was beaten. 'So it was a silly idea! Go ahead; laugh at me if you want! I just thought that…'

She made to slam the magazine shut, only to have the movement stilled abruptly as Amir suddenly reached out, closing strong fingers over her hand.

'What makes you think I'm laughing at you?'

'Well, you have to be. You can't possibly be taking this seriously! I just wanted to put a bit of romance into this and you—'

'And I promised you the affair of a lifetime,' Amir inserted quietly, but with an ominous edge to his voice that froze her when she would have struggled, trying to throw off his imprisoning grip. 'Lydia, look at me...'

Stubbornly she kept her face averted, still unable to look into his eyes. She no longer knew which she feared most. That he would be laughing, finding her amusing, even ridiculous. Or that he wouldn't. And suddenly somehow the thought of Amir being deadly serious about this turned her blood to ice, freezing in her veins.

'Lydia, I said look at me.'

His chair scraped on the floor as he pushed it back and stood up, leaning across the table towards her.

His hand came under her chin, lifting it determinedly. For a second she thought about resisting, but even as the thought slid into her mind his grip tightened warningly. Rather than face an undignified struggle that she knew she must inevitably lose, she flung her head back sharply, looking him right in the face, defiant blue eyes clashing with ruthless black.

'Do I look as if I'm laughing?'

'Well, no,' Lydia had to admit.

He had never looked more stern—or appeared more awe-inspiring, she admitted to herself. He hadn't spoken loudly or harshly—he hadn't needed to. Just the sound of that clear, cold voice was enough to douse the tiny flame of rebellion even as it flared inside her mind. And none of the movements he had made had been fast or hard or even faintly cruel, but it had been enough to make her let any idea of struggle die unformed and submit to his determined control.

'You look deadly serious.'

'That's because I am. Because if this is what you want, then it's what I want too.'

It was shocking how much she wanted to believe him. How much she wanted every word to be meant, to be deeply sincere. But what was even more disturbing was the realisation that even if he didn't truly mean it, she didn't care.

For the three days she had, she was perfectly willing to suspend disbelief. She was quite prepared to accept that if he said something was so, then it *was* so, even if under other circumstances she would be totally sceptical of his assertion. Amir could claim that he adored her, that he worshipped at her feet, and for these seventy-two hours she would take his word as gospel. She didn't care if she was deceiving herself, if she was laying herself open to every sort of con trick it was possible to play. It was what she wanted right now.

After all, he was only doing it to keep her here and involved, to keep her sweet. And the frightening, the dangerous thing was that he didn't need to do any of it. She couldn't *be* any more sweet on him, any more involved. He'd swept her right off her feet in the first moment she'd seen him and she had had no chance at all of regaining her balance ever since.

'I just thought it would be fun.'

'And it could be. But I think what we have to do is to backtrack here a little bit, fit in the stages that we missed out by jumping straight in with our eyes closed. Things like...'

He considered the article, running his finger down the list of events.

'Like you taking my phone number and saying you'll call?' Lydia sounded sceptical. 'Don't you think we're past that?'

'Maybe, maybe not. What is your number anyway?'

'You don't—' she began, then broke off as he turned a gently reproving look on her.

'You wanted to do this,' he reminded her.

'Oh, okay.'

Automatically she recited the number of her mobile, though as he didn't note it down she didn't quite see the point.

'I'd like to do this again,' he said unexpectedly, looking deep into her eyes as he spoke. 'I'll give you a call, some time. Would you like that?'

Too much.

She was in danger of actually saying it. She even opened her mouth to let the words out when panic screamed at her not to be so stupid. Amir was only playing the game, going along with the fantasy she had created. She would be every kind of a fool to place any trust in what he did.

'You—you do that,' she managed unevenly. 'That number will get me any time.'

Just for a swift, anguished second, she suddenly had a vivid idea of how it might have been if things had been different, if she and Amir had met under other circumstances. Her heart kicked sharply on an echo of how she might have felt then at the thought that this devastating man actually wanted to see her again. It might have been weak-willed, naïve in the extreme, but she knew she would have spent every night on edge, just waiting, willing the phone to ring, longing to hear his voice.

She didn't like to consider how she would have felt if she'd never heard from him again.

'So now we've done that one.'

With a firm, decisive sweep of the pen, Amir ticked off the item on the list in the magazine.

'What can we do next? Oh, yes, we were going shopping.'

'No, we're not.'

If she had felt uncomfortable about it before, she felt a

hundred times worse now. Letting Amir buy her clothes, providing her with what amounted to a brand-new wardrobe, seemed to come with too many strings attached.

His sigh was a deliberate blend of annoyance and resigned patience.

'Do you ever do anything without arguing?' he demanded impatiently.

'I told you what I wanted.'

'So you did.'

His mouth twisted, the gleam of a dangerously explosive temper only just reined in burning in his eyes.

'But you can't just change the rules when it pleases you.'

'Rules? What rules? I…Oh-h-h!'

The words shrivelled on her tongue as Amir tapped the open magazine with an imperious finger.

'Stage Ten—you buy each other presents,' read the heading. 'You're crazy about each other and you want to show it. You feel totally extravagant and money is very definitely no object.'

'You see,' Amir put in silkily, murmuring the words against her ear, his cheek resting on her hair as she stared down at the words. 'I'm supposed to buy you presents. And the more extravagant, the better.'

But the extravagance of the presents was supposed to indicate the depth of his feelings for her. It was not just to compensate for the inadequacies of the clothing she had brought with her and ensure that she didn't have to wear the same sweater and jeans day in and day out for the next seventy-two hours.

'But I can't return the favour!'

What did one buy for a man who had everything? A man who was a Crown Prince, whose father was a *sheikh*?

'I can't buy you—'

'Lady, there's nothing you could buy me that I'd want any more than what you've already given me.'

Another day, another time, it might have been different. If he'd had another sort of future ahead of him, if his life had been at a different set of crossroads, then maybe there would have been something she could offer him. But not now.

'Lady, there's nothing you could buy me that I'd want…'

Cold and curt and stark, the words took her breath away. She had to bite down hard on her lower lip to drive back the cry of pain that almost escaped her. He had had what he wanted and there was nothing more she could give him.

'So, do we go out and choose some clothes?' Amir hadn't noticed her withdrawal, or if he had he was deliberately ignoring it.

'Okay.' She couldn't look him in the face, couldn't meet his eyes. 'I'll just clear up here.'

'Jamila can do that.'

'Amir, you may be used to having servants, but I'm not. I made the mess, I'll tidy it up!'

'Then I—' Amir began but out in the hallway the shrill ring of the telephone drew his attention.

'You get that,' Lydia told him. 'I'll finish in here.'

She wouldn't think about it, she told herself fiercely as she cleared the table, putting things in the dishwasher. She just wouldn't let herself brood on the fact that she had already given Amir the one, the only thing he wanted from her.

This wasn't a lifetime sort of thing. She had given herself three days out of reality just to enjoy this experience— to enjoy being with Amir. She wouldn't ask for anything else. She couldn't even let herself dream that there was the hope of anything else. To do so was to risk the total desolation of heartbreak when the end came.

She would accept this for what it was and nothing more. She was just drying her hands carefully when a sudden sound startled her. For a second she couldn't quite work out what it was, then it registered.

Her phone! Someone was calling her phone.

Hurrying to her bag, she picked it up and studied the number displayed. It wasn't one she recognised. In fact it was one she was absolutely certain she hadn't seen in her life before. Burning with curiosity, she thumbed the 'on' button.

'Hello?'

'Hi!'

It was Amir's voice, deep and husky, the faint trace of his accent highlighted and deepened by the receiver.

'I said I'd give you a call…'

'So you did.'

She was deeply thankful that he couldn't see her and so was unaware of the hot colour that rushed into her face, the sudden jerky beat of her heart, the way her eyes suddenly lit from within.

This was how it would have felt if this had been a real relationship. How she would have reacted if she'd waited around, dreaming of his call, willing him to phone. And then, like now, she would have tried to pay it cool, tried to pretend that it was no big deal, that she hadn't been waiting—not much anyway.

'What was it you wanted?'

'I wondered if you were free tonight? If you'd like to do something—a meal—a film maybe.'

'What is this, Amir?'

Lydia dropped all the pretence, unable to maintain it any longer.

'What are you doing?'

'Don't you know?'

Amusement threaded through the deep voice, enriching it with honey.

'Stage Five—comes after Stage Three— ''He takes your

number and says he'll give you a call.'' And Stage Four—
''You wait in all week and he never phones.'''

Unable to resist a swift, stunned glance at the phone as
if were was actually Amir's face, Lydia bit her lip sharply.
How did he know? Had he actually been reading her mind?

'Stage Five,' Amir repeated. '''Just when you've given
up hope he finally rings and asks you for a date.'''

'And is that what you're doing? Asking me out on a
date?'

'Don't you think it's about time?' The amusement in
the husky voice had deepened. 'Like I said, it's time we
backtracked to Stage Five after rushing ahead to Stages
Twelve and Eighteen before we should. So—what about
tonight?'

'I—I don't know.'

What was the point? she wanted to ask. Why should
Amir bother to take her out on a date when he knew all
the time—they both knew—that at the end of the evening
she would be coming straight back here?

And weren't dates all about courtship, anticipation, enticement? Amir didn't have to bother with any of those.
He didn't need to wonder if she might end up in his bed.
He knew she had no choice. It was part of the bargain they
had made.

'I'm not sure…'

'Oh, I see,' Amir interrupted smoothly. 'You've moved
on to Six.'

The amusement was still there in his voice but this time
it was shaded with a darker note, one that made her nerves
twist to hear it.

'Playing hard to get?' Lydia's laugh was ragged at the
edges. 'I thought that was expected of me—if we're playing by the rules. But perhaps we'd better stop—'

'Lady, you started this.' Amir's voice was a low growl
down the phone. 'You can't back out now. We're not even

halfway through. You wanted that ''super-sexy affair'', so that's what you're going to get...'

But she'd been half joking, saying something only to cover up the nervousness she'd felt.

'You—you *mean* it?'

'I mean it,' Amir affirmed brusquely. 'Over the next three days you're going to get all of those ''sensual stages''. Every damn one of them.'

It was frankly scary how much he did mean it, he admitted to himself as he switched off his phone. He had started out meaning to convince her and had ended up convincing himself.

No, that wasn't strictly true. He hadn't taken that much convincing. In fact, he'd been up for it from the start. The whole silly, crazy idea had grabbed him in a way that nothing had done for a long, long time. It wasn't real, it was just play, pure fantasy, but fantasy was something his life had been missing for as long as he could remember. It had been nothing but hard work, determination and commitment. And the future that was planned out looked like going that way too.

Maybe now was time to play a little. He had this unexpected interval between one world, one life and another. Maybe he could snatch a little unplanned fun before the doors of reality closed again.

CHAPTER EIGHT

'BUT I don't need it!'

'Do you really think that matters?'

Amir's tone was one of resigned tolerance, but, sensitive to everything about him, Lydia caught the thread of impatience that warned of his temper fraying round the edges. It was almost frightening how well she knew him already, how easily she could judge his frame of mind, predict his changes of mood.

For most of the day he had been in a generous, expansive humour, spending money on her in a way that was almost shocking. She had very quickly learned not to pause to look at something, not to pick it up to admire, because if she did then Amir would have bought it for her before she could blink, adding yet another item to the growing collection of parcels that he wanted delivered back to the apartment.

But this dress was different. This dress was ridiculously expensive, even for the exclusive designer boutique they were in. It was also impossibly glamorous, the sort of dress she had never worn in her life, and one that she was never going to have a chance to wear in the future. Certainly not in the three days that she was to be with Amir.

'Do you like it?'

'How could anyone *not* like it?'

Turning round again, she contemplated her reflection in the full-length mirror, finding it impossible to believe that it was actually her.

In a lavender blue silk, the dress had a softly draped skirt and tight-fitting bodice, supported by thin, shoestring straps. Tiny beads of crystal were scattered across the delicate material, giving the impression that raindrops had just fallen onto it, pooling softly.

The colour did amazing things for her eyes, and the perfect fit and design made her look taller and slimmer than ever, the low-cut neckline framing the fine bone structure of her shoulders and neck, the soft curves of the tops of her breasts.

'I love it!'

'Then it's yours.'

'No!'

She swung back to where the man who had been at her side like a dark, sexy shadow all day now lounged indolently in the chair provided by the manageress, hands linked behind his head, black eyes lazily hooded.

'It's too expensive and I'll never wear it!'

'The cost is a pittance and you'll need it for number twenty-four.'

'Amir!'

Lydia actually stamped her foot in frustration at the way he wasn't listening, earning herself a quick, surprised glance from the saleswoman hovering nearby. The older woman obviously thought that she was quite, quite mad and had been of that opinion from the start. Why else would Lydia argue the toss at every turn, trying to dissuade this obviously indulgent lover from buying any more than the basics when he was clearly intent on lavishing a small fortune on her?

'Just *what* is number twenty-four?'

'Wouldn't you like to know?' he drawled teasingly, lightly touching one long-fingered hand to the inside pocket of his superbly cut jacket.

The faint rustle of paper under the soft, supple suede reminded Lydia of the way that, just before they had left the house, he had suddenly turned back, hurrying into the kitchen. Standing waiting by the door, she had heard the sound of tearing paper and as Amir had joined her once more he had been folding a couple of brightly coloured sheets into four.

'What's that?' she had asked in some surprise.

'The agenda for the next couple of days—the ''Sensual Stages'',' he'd elaborated when she'd frowned her incomprehension. 'We have to make sure we don't miss anything out.'

'Twenty-four?'

Now Lydia tried hard to recall just what other 'stages' she had seen, but number twenty-four eluded her, particularly when Amir lifted an autocratic hand, summoning the saleswoman to his side.

'We'll take this,' he said. 'And the rest...'

A casual gesture indicated other dresses, tops, skirts and trousers that Lydia had tried on earlier and which now hung on a rack on the other side of the room.

'Amir, no!' Lydia protested, horrified at the thought of the amount he had spent on her.

'Amir—*yes*!' he contradicted. 'Remember number ten—as extravagant as possible.'

She opened her mouth to argue further but one swift, reproving look from those brilliant dark eyes had her closing it again with a snap. It hadn't taken her long to learn that with Amir there was a line drawn very firmly to indicate just how far he would let her go. She could go right up to that line if she wanted, even put her toe on the outermost edge of it, and he would let her get away with it. But step over the line, by so much as an inch, and she was inviting instant and devastating retribution.

She'd learned that lesson earlier that day. They had stopped for a meal in an elegant restaurant and, lulled into a sense of false security by the relaxed ease Amir had shown until then, she had tried to satisfy her curiosity about him. She was involved so closely with this man in one way, had been totally intimate with him, known and touched every part of his body, let him kiss and caress hers in return, and yet she knew so little about him in others.

Over the meal he had asked her about her family, her life before she had won the job in California, and, inspired by his ability to listen, she had told him. He had a special way of making her feel that she were the only person in the room, so that it had all come pouring out without hesitation. She had told him about her parents, her first job as a trainee in the small, provincial hotel then, later, as Hospitality Manager in a four-star hotel in Leicester. With pride in her eyes, she'd recounted how she'd been headhunted for the California job, the stringent interviews she'd gone through to win it.

She'd told him everything about herself, even the uncomfortable story of Jonathon and his rejection of her. And so while they'd lingered over coffee, she'd felt that it had finally been his turn.

'And what about you?' she asked impulsively. 'What about your family? Isn't it time you told me about your father—the sheikh? If he's really your father, how come you speak such perfect English?'

Amir set his cup down on its saucer with a cold precision that later, looking back, she realised that she should have seen as the first hint of warning. But at the time, relaxed and content after a wonderful meal and a glass of wine, she didn't notice the immediate withdrawal, the storm brewing behind his dark eyes.

'My mother was English,' he said. 'And I was brought up in England.'

'Your mother didn't live with your father, then?'

'They separated when I was eighteen months old.'

'Oh, what a pity! Why?'

This time the danger signs were more overt; the tension in the strong jaw, the way his hand tightened over his teaspoon, were enough to make her realise she should proceed with caution.

'He believed that she had been unfaithful to her.'

It was still there, he realised with something of a shock. The pain, the sense of betrayal, wasn't locked away as securely as he had thought, but lingered just out of sight, easily revived again by a careless question.

'He didn't trust her enough. And he was too old-fashioned, too entrenched in the old ways of doing things that he couldn't see it was possible for a woman to have a male friend without something underhand going on.'

'Oh, how sad! But I'm surprised that he let you go with her. I would have thought that he would have wanted to keep his son…'

Amir dropped the teaspoon onto the table with a distinct clatter. He had thought that too, once. He had believed that his father wouldn't willingly have let him go or that, having had his hand forced, he would at least have been ready to welcome his son back with open arms.

He was uncomfortable with this line of conversation. He had promised himself this space between his two lives without the taint of the past darkening and spoiling it. His father had done that more than enough.

'Why—?'

'Lydia, that's enough!'

'But—'

'I said *that's enough*.'

'I just—'

She didn't even get a chance to form the sentence.

'I'm leaving,' he announced baldly. 'Are you coming or not?'

A tiny signal, so brief she hardly saw it, brought the waiter hovering nearby. With the bill paid, and without another word, Amir pushed back his chair and stood up. A moment later, he had turned his back on her and was marching across the room, heading for the exit. Not by so much as a gesture or a look did he give any indication of any interest in whether she followed him or not. It was only when she realised that he fully intended to walk away completely, leaving her behind without a second thought, that she saw she would have to hurry to catch him up if she was not to lose him for good.

'Wait for me!' she complained. 'Amir, I can't keep up with you at this pace!'

The burning look he shot at her from beneath the lush black lashes seemed to say that he didn't give a damn whether she kept up with him or not.

'What brought all this on? I only asked the same sort of questions you asked me. I didn't know it was a state secret! Nothing to start World War Three about.'

'Don't be silly!'

What *was* he doing? He hadn't wanted his father's malign influence to taint this brief idyll, and yet that was exactly what he was letting happen.

'I'm sorry,' he said stiffly. 'I don't want to talk about my family. They're not relevant to here and now—to you and me.'

To *you and me*.

He couldn't have said anything more calculated to stop her dead in her tracks. It even made her push aside the memory of that curt, 'I'm sorry', a response that had been tossed at her so harshly and so indifferently that it hardly merited the name of an apology at all.

And then he did something that made her forget the argument and all that had led up to it. After a swift glance at the clock, he reached into his pocket and pulled out a slim, gift-wrapped parcel.

'Now's the time to give you this. Happy anniversary.'

'Anniversary?'

'It's exactly twenty-four hours since we first spoke to each other—our first anniversary.'

His gift was on her wrist now. A slender gold watch that when she had opened it had been set to exactly the time of their meeting. Another present to add to the growing pile of things he had showered on her. Things she wasn't even sure she wanted.

But *you and me*. She wanted that. Oh, dear God, it was scary how *much* she wanted that! And the realisation of just what it meant to her stilled her impetuous tongue, and froze the angry protest on her lips.

They had so little time together. She didn't want to waste any of it arguing with him. She would only regret it later, when the three days he had allowed her were up, and she could no longer see or talk to him again.

And so she forced a smile onto her face, made herself meet those stunning eyes with a confidence she was far from feeling.

'Number ten it is, then.'

The smile became more genuine as she glanced into the saleslady's face, saw the stunned look in her eyes. By the time they had left the shop she couldn't hold back the giggles any longer.

'Did you see that woman's expression? Number ten, twenty-four indeed! She probably thought we were talking about positions in bed—that we were planning an orgy!'

'Then she was reading my mind,' Amir returned in a voice made husky by desire. The dark-eyed glance he shot her sizzled all the way from her head to her toes in a single, sweeping survey. 'Because that's exactly what I was thinking.'

And as soon as he said the words, that was exactly what she was thinking of too. Images that were positively indecent in a public street flooded her thoughts, heating her blood and making her pulse thud heavily in her veins. In spite of the fact that it had now begun to snow again and that the darkness of a freezing winter evening was already beginning to close in on them, she felt as if she were burning up with some raging fever, her clothes too rough against her suddenly sensitised skin.

'Me too,' she murmured, the sharp excitement of anticipation putting a shake into her voice.

'So...'

Amir snaked an arm around her waist, pulling her into the shelter of his tall, strong body as they moved off down the street.

'Do you have any more shopping to do?'

Lydia slanted a flirtatious, beguiling look up into his dark face.

'None at all.'

'So we can go home now?'

Home. It struck at her heart like a blow, driving all the air from her lungs in a shocked gasp. The apartment was home to Amir, but it would never be any such thing to her.

For the next three days it would be where she lived, where she ate, slept. Where she made love with Amir. But at the end of those three days she would pack her bags and leave and she would never see the apartment or Amir again.

'Amir...'

She choked out his name on a wave of distress, looking up into his shadowed face, seeing the way that the street lights, the glow from the shop windows illuminated those carved cheekbones, the brilliant eyes. And her heart clenched on a stab of pain as she suddenly realised just what was happening to her.

'Amir... This isn't working.'

It was obviously the last thing he had anticipated and she saw his proud head go back, saw the sudden flash of something raw, something unshielded in his eyes.

'What?' If his voice had been husky before, now it was hoarse with shock. 'What the hell's brought this on? *Why* isn't it working?'

There was no answer she could give. She couldn't even give herself one. Not unless she put into words the half-formed idea that had just exploded in her mind, shattering her thoughts and driving her into a numb sense of shock.

'Oh, don't ask me that, Amir!'

'And why not?'

To her consternation he came to a dead halt in the middle of the pavement, heedless of the mutters of disapproval from the other pedestrians who almost cannoned into him as he swung her round to face him.

'Don't ask!' he echoed savagely. 'Don't you think that at least you owe me some sort of explanation, not just "This isn't working"?'

Lydia flinched away from the ferocity of his question, shrinking into the upturned collar of her coat, hunching her shoulders against the force of his attack.

'*Why* is it not working? We had an arrangement—you agreed to it. Am I not fulfilling what you expected? What more is there you want?'

And there it was, Lydia thought drearily. There was the whole crux of the situation, the core of the problem. With the incisiveness of a brutally sharp knife, Amir had gone straight to the heart of what was troubling her—straight to *her heart*, which was where the problem lay.

'What more is there you want?'

He meant what more could he give her in the way of material things, and the real problem was that what she needed was *emotional* and that was something he was never going to give her.

'Amir,' she protested edgily. 'You're blocking the pavement; getting in people's way.'

His retort was short, succinct and extremely forceful, showing just how little he cared for the people who passed them by, heads turning in curiosity at the sight of the two of them standing still in the middle of what was now swiftly turning into a whirling blizzard.

'I want to know what's bugging you,' he insisted. 'Just what's going on in that lovely head of yours? And I don't intend to move from here until you tell me. So unless you plan on staying here all night, you'd better start talking—fast!'

Which was guaranteed to drive all coherent thought straight from her mind.

Except for one. And that was the realisation that had so shocked her only moments before that it had driven her into making that foolish declaration, and puzzling and infuriating Amir in equal measure, so that he had reacted as he had.

I think I'm falling in love with you.

It was the one thing she couldn't say. The one thing she *must not* say. It was the thing that Amir least wanted to hear; the fact that she absolutely did not want him to know.

Love was not part of their bargain. It had no place in the carefully defined and time-limited arrangement Amir had spelled out in the first place. And that arrangement was all he had to offer her; her part in it all he wanted from her.

'Lydia...'

Amir's tone warned that his patience was growing dangerously thin.

'Are you going to tell me, or do I have to drag it out of you? Two minutes ago you were as ready to go home as I was. You knew why—what I wanted, and it was what you wanted too. Wasn't it?—*Wasn't it?*' he demanded more sharply when she wouldn't meet the angry force of his eyes.

Lydia couldn't lie to him.

'Yes,' she admitted, shifting uneasily from one foot to another on the icy pavement.

'Then what changed your mind? Something I said or...'

The polished jet eyes went to the brightly lit window of the boutique they had just left. Behind the single display model in the window he could see the figure of the saleswoman busily packing away the clothes they had bought in layers of tissue paper before placing them in bronze-coloured cardboard boxes.

And suddenly he knew. He felt as if he had been kicked in the guts by the wild hind legs of a mule because it was so unexpected. He had been all sorts of a damn fool because for once he had actually been deceived. Somewhere along the line he had let down the powerful defences he normally kept carefully built up around his emotions and let this girl in.

He had forgotten about the lessons past experience had taught him and pushed aside the conviction that most women were only with him for what they could get. He had even allowed himself to believe that Lydia was different.

And now he had been proved wrong. And it hurt. It hurt badly.

'I see,' he said heavily. 'Oh, yes, lady. I see.'

'What?'

It was Lydia's turn to be bewildered, her eyes wide and stunned in the uneven light, the shadow patterns made by the whirling snow shifting and changing on her face.

'What do you see?'

Amir gave a nod of his dark head towards the shop they had just left.

'You have what you wanted, so now it "isn't working".'

The bitterness of his mimicry tore at her heart.

'You've got everything you thought there was on offer and now you're off.'

'No-o.'

It was finally beginning to dawn on Lydia just what he meant and her protest was a low moan of pain, barely audible above the wind.

'Yes,' Amir contradicted brutally. 'Yes, that's what you thought, my darling. What was going on in your scheming little mind. But let me tell you something, sweetheart…'

His tone turned the word into something that was light years away from any sort of endearment.

'You jumped too fast—made your play too early. Because that *wasn't* all I was going to give you. Not by a long way. You're going to kick yourself, darling, when you realise that if you'd just stuck around, stayed with me the three days we arranged—even one day more—then I would have—'

'*No!*'

Lydia couldn't bear it any longer. She couldn't listen to that brutal, cutting voice that lashed at her tender flesh like a whip, couldn't bear to see the bleak coldness of his eyes that looked straight through her as if she didn't really exist but was just a phantom, an image projected into the space in front of him.

'No, no, no! That isn't true! That isn't what it was like at all! Oh, Amir, *please*! You have to believe me!'

'No? Then what was it like, my lovely?'

The eyes he turned on her pale face were terrifyingly blank, all emotion drained out of them. Lydia had the sudden fearful thought that she would rather see something, anything at all, even if it was the burn of dangerous fury in those black depths. Anything, other than this opaque withdrawal.

But what could she say that didn't give her away and that he would believe?

'I—I just got frightened. It's all happened so fast. I've never experienced anything like this before.'

It was shocking how much he wanted to believe her. How he wanted to think that it was sincerity that burned in those pansy-dark eyes. That the pleading face she had turned up to his was genuine, and not just a play for his finer feelings. Either way it was working. He could feel the hurt anger start to ebb, leaving him bruised and wary.

The snow had soaked into her hair, flattening it around her finely shaped skull, and as he watched a tiny drop of water slipped from one dark strand and dropped onto her forehead. Slowly it slid over her skin, down towards her temple. Without thinking he put out a hand and caught it, wiping it away before it could fall into one of those bright blue eyes.

The tiny contact froze them both where they stood, eyes locking together, his breathing almost stopped.

'Amir!' Lydia murmured. 'Please…'

And suddenly he knew he didn't care. He didn't give a damn whether she was on the make or not. He'd promised himself three days and then she was leaving anyway. Just how much could she take from him in that short time?

And he wanted all of those three days. Wanted them more than he had ever wanted anything in the world. Even the need for his father's recognition hadn't been as fierce and strong as this, raging like a fire through his guts, twisting in every nerve.

'I got scare—' Lydia began but he didn't want her to talk any more.

The heavy pulse of desire was pounding through his veins, making it impossible to think. He was only aware of one thing, and that was the growing hunger, the insistent demand of his body. He didn't want *words*.

And so he laid one long forefinger across the softness of her lips, silencing her while his impenetrable gaze still held hers totally transfixed.

'Don't talk,' he said harshly. 'Not another word. We're wasting time with this. Time we don't have. All I want from you is two more days of your life. Two days and at the end of that we go our separate ways. You thought you could manage that this morning, so what's changed? Surely you can make it ''work'' for as long as that.'

It was that 'two more days' that did it. Just as it had when he had originally offered her the suggestion that they had just three days and three nights together when she had thought there would only be a one-night stand. So now the realisation that they only had two of those days left shocked her into knowing that she couldn't give them up, no matter what.

'Yes,' she whispered, shaken and low. 'Yes, I can manage that.'

'Then come here...'

He held his arms out to her and like a small, frightened animal seeking shelter she went into them willingly and eagerly. She felt his grip close around her, tight as steel bands, crushing her against the fine material of his overcoat, and it was like coming home.

One strong hand came under her chin, pushing her face up to meet his, and he took her mouth with a burning passion that made her head swim, a low moan of surrender escaping her immediately.

She wasn't aware of how long they stayed there, lips locked together, his tongue plundering the inner sweetness of her mouth, oblivious to the bitter fury of the weather or the amused glances of a dozen or more passers-by. She only knew that when he finally lifted his head, touched his lips to her forehead, and enveloped her in a fierce hug that crushed against the hard warmth of his body, she could find no strength to argue any further.

So when he said in a voice that was rough and thick with the passion that had them both in its grip, '*Now* we go home,' she could only nod in silent agreement. She couldn't think of any reason to object. Couldn't even recall why she had wanted to do such a crazy thing in the first place.

Managing the next two days with him, making that work, was the easy part.

It was the going their separate ways at the end of it that she couldn't bear to think about.

CHAPTER NINE

'SO, WHAT else is left on that crazy list of yours?'

Amir was lounging back in his chair in the sitting room, a mug of coffee in one hand and the morning paper open on his lap.

'How many more stages have we left undone?'

'Let's see…'

Lydia unfolded the pages from the magazine and smoothed them out. They were beginning to look rather worn now, crumpled and creased from being crushed inside Amir's pocket and then taken out again, and with many of the stages crossed off over the past day and a half.

'Meeting, phoning, first date…'

All of those had been checked off, and more.

Just for a moment she paused, her thoughts going back to the night before, after Amir had brought her back from the shops.

The short journey to the apartment had seemed impossibly long and unendurable. The atmosphere in the back of Amir's car, with Nabil silent and impervious in the driver's seat, had been so heated, so thick with desire, that she'd hardly been able to breathe. Under cover of the darkness, Amir had taken her into his arms and kissed her demandingly, crushing her mouth open under his, bending her head back against the iron support of his arm.

And when he had finished with her mouth he had trailed his lips along the burning line of her cheek, then up to the delicate curve of her ear. And there he'd lingered, whispering to her of the plans he'd had for when they got home, the things he'd wanted to do to her, with her, for her, until she'd been writhing on the leather covered seat in an agony of excited anticipation, unable to bear the waiting until they'd been alone together again.

It had been every bit as electrifying as he had promised. From the moment that the door had slammed behind them and they'd been alone in the darkness of the hall, he had taken her into his arms again and subjected her to a sensual onslaught that had set her head spinning, her pulse thundering, and her breath coming in ragged, uneven gasps.

She'd been as hungry and impatient as she had been the first night, pulling at his clothes, wrenching his shirt open, pressing starving kisses against the hot satin of his skin. But Amir had been in a very different mood this time.

His seduction of her had been slow, enticing, totally sensual. He'd drawn out each kiss, each caress into long, agonising seconds, stroking and smoothing, tantalising until she'd been moaning under his touch, begging him to hurry.

'Hurry?'

The word was a husky laugh in her ear.

'Oh, no, my darling, not this time. Last night we couldn't wait. We didn't know how long we had and we had to cram as much as we possibly could into the space we had available. Tonight we have all the time in the world.'

This time their journey up the stairs was a slow, gentle progress. On each step he paused and kissed her, caressed her some more. And when they reached the landing he caught her up in his arms, carried her into the bedroom where he laid her softly on the bed and came down beside her. Pulling her close to him, he stroked her hair, smoothing it back from her face, following the touch of his hand with yet more burning kisses.

Her cheek rested against the fine material of his shirt, supported on the lean, hard wall of his chest, rising and falling with every deep, even breath that he took. Only the heavy pounding of his heart, beating as urgently as her own, gave away the fact that he was as aroused as she was, fighting as hard for control.

With a soft touch and even softer words he eased her clothes from her body, muttering thickly in the language of his father as he peeled away the tight jeans, the wisps of silk and lace that were her underwear.

'This is what works between us,' he told her between fierce, crushing kisses. 'We don't need to follow lists or magazine articles to ensure we've got this right.'

She welcomed the hard thrust of his forcefully aroused body into her, willing the pleasure it created to drive away all the doubts and fears that had bombarded her earlier that afternoon. This was what she wanted. This wild, blazing passion that erased thought, stopped worry and made her feel that there could be nothing better in the whole, wide world. With his arms tight around her, the strength of his body crushing her, she couldn't think of anything beyond him, and that was exactly how she wanted it to be.

'Some of these we're going to have to forget about,' she said now, frowning down at the magazine article in her hand.

'You think so?'

Amir stretched lazily, running both hands through the black silk of his hair. 'And why is that?'

'Well, it's hardly going to be possible to organise Christmas in February, is it? It's a little early for Valentine's Day, and my birthday isn't till the fourteenth of June.'

'Well, perhaps we'll find something to put in their place,' Amir told her, getting up in a single, elegantly fluid movement and strolling to the window to frown out at the scene in the street below. 'Though if this snow doesn't let up, we could well be stuck here until April, still waiting for the airports to open.'

A note in his voice caught Lydia very much on the raw.

'And that wouldn't please you, of course!'

Her retort had him swinging round to face her, earning her a reproving frown and an angry glare.

'What makes you say that?'

When he was in this mood, he was pure sheikh of the desert, Crown Prince of Kuimar from his head to his toes, Lydia told herself, tensing warily, preparing for the lash of his temper. It was easy to imagine him dressed, not in the Western clothes of casual jeans and loose shirt, but in the formal, flowing robes of his heritage. In her mind's eye she could picture him, tall and proud, striding across the desert of his homeland. Lord of all he surveyed.

'Why would it not please me?'

'Well, it would keep you from whatever you must get to in three—two now—days' time. It must be something very important.'

'It is.'

Well, she'd asked for that, Lydia admitted. In fact she'd gone down on her knees and begged for it, reminding him that his affair with her was strictly temporary. Not that he'd shown any sign of forgetting that fact, of course. His first action this morning had been to check with the airport again, even though a further fall of snow had made it highly unlikely that the planes were going to take off at any time today.

He couldn't have done anything more calculated to remind her that her time with him was strictly limited, and that he had no intention of changing his mind about that fact. And it hurt—terribly.

When he had slid from the bed and headed for the phone as soon as he had woken, she had stayed totally still, trying to pretend that she'd still been asleep so that she hadn't had to face him until she had gathered some degree of composure. At least keeping her eyes closed had held back the sting of tears that she'd refused to let herself shed. She hadn't felt that she'd been able to cope with the questions that would inevitably have followed.

'And you knew that before we started on this.' Amir's voice was harsh with angry reproof. 'So don't start telling me you're having second thoughts now.'

'Me? Second thoughts?'

The struggle to hide her pain made her voice high and brittle in a way that obviously displeased him. Another of those dark, disapproving frowns had her bringing it down an octave hastily.

'Not at all. But I was beginning to wonder if perhaps you had.'

'About ending this after three days?'

The look he turned on her made her heart shrink. It was just as well she hadn't been fool enough to mean that question the way he'd taken it. If she had even so much as entertained the hope that he was reconsidering his edict that after three days it was all over between them, then that fierce glare would have destroyed her dream in a second.

'No, not that! I was just thinking that perhaps you didn't even want to wait that long. You rang the airport last night and again first thing this morning.'

'I thought you had a job to go to.'

'Well, yes—I do…'

Clearly now was not the time to tell him that if he only said the word, if he asked her to stay, if he spoke one syllable of love she would reconsider her trip to California at once.

No, she didn't even need the word 'love'. Fool that she was, she was already in so deep that if he had simply said he wanted her to stick around, that he hadn't tired of her, she would have been tempted to stay.

But clearly Amir had no thoughts of saying any such thing.

'And I have commitments elsewhere.'

'What sort of commitments?'

No, Lydia! That was quite the wrong thing to ask. If he wanted you to know, then he would have said. He would have told you from the first!

But to her surprise Amir actually offered some sort of an answer.

'I'm travelling to Kuimar just as soon as the jet can leave.'

Somehow that didn't have quite the same ring in his mind as it had done forty-eight hours ago, Amir registered with a sense of shock. Two days ago he had been totally convinced, totally at ease with the decision he had made. Now he felt as if that certainty had been eroded from within. He no longer felt quite so comfortable with the plans his father had made for the future.

'My father is expecting me.'

He was more than expecting. The old man had sent out a royal decree and he had no doubt that it would be obeyed.

'And you have to go?'

'*Yes*, I have to go.'

He spoke with more force than he intended. Sometimes it seemed as if she came dangerously close to reading his mind. She had an uncanny knack of putting her finger right on the point that was fretting at his thoughts and aggravating the unease it was causing.

'More than that. I *want* to go. Kuimar is my country. I belong there even if I didn't grow up there as a child.'

'Why was that? Why didn't you grow up there?'

She wished the question back as soon as it slipped out. It was obvious that he'd said more than he'd ever intended and she was afraid that her impulsive query would drive him back behind the barriers he erected between her and the life he considered so private.

To her surprise he came prowling back across the room

to throw himself into the soft leather armchair he had left just moments before.

'When my father divorced my mother for being unfaithful, he also disowned me. He believed that I was not his son but the child of the man she had had an affair with. For years he would have nothing to do with either of us. That's why I grew up in England. As a matter of fact, my father only actually acknowledged me as his son two years ago.'

'I can't even begin to think how that must have felt. For both you and your mother.'

Amir's mouth twisted bitterly, his dark eyes staring broodingly down at a spot on the carpet.

'My mother died without ever being reconciled with my father. For years he totally ignored the fact that I existed—even when our paths were forced to cross.'

'How...?'

The twist to that sensual mouth grew more pronounced.

'I breed and train racehorses. My father's greatest obsession, after his country, is steeplechasing. But even if we were in the same paddock together he wouldn't even acknowledge my presence.'

'Oh, Amir!'

She wanted to go to him, to hold him, to say something, however inadequate, to show her sympathy. But the cold, set mask that was his face, the stiff, unyielding way he held his long body, all declared clearly, without words, that he would reject the gesture if she tried to make it. The barriers were firmly in place; the 'Keep out' signs ruthlessly displayed.

'What changed his mind?'

That jet-eyed gaze flicked up just once to sear her skin in a burning, savage flare of anger.

'His other wives did not provide him with the sons he wanted. Unfortunately for my father, all his other children have been female. In the end his hand was forced by the restlessness in the country because he didn't have an heir. He agreed to abide by the results of DNA testing.'

'He couldn't accept you without that!'

'My sweet Lydia—there was a throne and a country at stake. If I had been an impostor, it would have dishonoured his line for ever.'

'But didn't you...?'

'I did what had to be done,' Amir told her simply.

He didn't have to tell her what a blow to his pride it had been. It was there in his eyes, in the hard set of his jaw, the tension etched into the muscles of his face. She was beginning to see just why he was so determined to join his father in Kuimar as soon as he could. He had fought so hard for his place as the prince of that country, now that he had it he wasn't going to take any chances with losing it, whatever it took.

And that put her securely in her place, she told herself miserably. She was relegated to a position of no importance, no consequence in Amir's life, to be used for his pleasure and then discarded. After all, what did she have to set against the attractions of a whole country—a *kingdom* where one day he would rule as Sheikh?

She would do far better to end it now. It would hurt terribly, but sooner the anguish of a clean break than the slow death by letting the relationship fray and disintegrate into nothingness.

She had opened her mouth to declare as much, to tell Amir that she couldn't go on when a ring at the doorbell startled her.

'What's that?'

Unexpectedly Amir's cold expression had lightened. There was a new gleam in his eye, even the hint of a smile curving the corners of his mouth.

'Why don't you go and see?'

'But it won't be anyone for me. No one knows...'

'Go and see!'

It was a royal command, delivered in a tone that allowed for no thought of disobeying, so that Lydia got to her feet in a rush and hurried to the door without any further question.

'Miss Lydia Ashton? We have a delivery for you.'

'For me—but…'

Words failed her as she saw the huge bouquet of red, scented roses in the delivery man's hands. And behind him was another man carrying a matching bouquet…and another…and another…

Lydia fell back against the wall, unable to speak a word. Incapable of doing anything but waving them vaguely in the direction of the kitchen to deposit the flowers on the table. It was only when Amir appeared, providing a generous tip and ushering them out again, that she regained the use of her tongue.

'Did you do this?'

His grin was wide and wicked in its delight at her consternation.

'Number fourteen—appropriately enough,' he told her. 'Happy Valentine's Day, Lydia. *Our* Valentine's Day, anyway.'

It was the beginning of a day that blew Lydia's mind completely, leaving her incapable of thought, of reason, and eventually of any words at all.

She had said that in order to fit in all the 'sensual stages' mapped out in the magazine, she thought they would have to cram things up a bit, but she had never anticipated this! The day was a whirlwind of experiences, of sensations that came at her thick and fast until her mind was spinning dizzily.

Valentine's Day came first, with the roses, cards, a silk nightdress and negligée wrapped in silver paper. A couple of hours later, it was 'Easter'.

The biggest, most luxurious, Swiss chocolate egg she had ever seen was delivered to the door, along with armfuls of toys in the shape of fluffy yellow chicks and smooth white furry rabbits and finally baskets of primroses, daffodils, and tulips to fill every space where there wasn't already a huge bunch of roses.

'Amir!' she protested weakly, a shaken edge of laughter in her voice. 'This is crazy! You must have bought up a whole florist's shop—and a toyshop, come to that! And as for that Easter egg…'

'Are you telling me that you don't like chocolate?' Amir enquired, a teasing light dancing in his ebony eyes.

'No—I love it! But no one person could ever eat their way through a quarter of that.'

'Then you'll have to have some help.'

His smile grew wider, more vivid, deliberately enticing.

'I never intended that you should have it all to yourself. I did have plans to share it with you.'

They shared it in bed.

It started with Amir feeding her slivers of the sinfully rich confection as he had fed her the ripe peach on their first evening together. Later, Lydia found a childlike delight in tracing intricate patterns over Amir's golden skin using the deeper shade of the chocolate before she licked it off with a delicate care that had him groaning in erotic response. Later still they made love with the sweetness lingering on their lips, combining with the swirl of tongues, the intimate, intensely personal taste of each others' skin in a potently erotic cocktail.

And as they lay in bed afterwards, their breath gradually slowing, the slick sheen of sweat drying on their love weary bodies, Amir reached for the pages of the magazine that detailed the list he had been following.

'Valentine's. Easter…'

His rich deep voice was thick with satisfaction as he ticked them off.

'What's next?'

'Next?' Lydia groaned in disbelief. 'Amir, you can't be

serious! You've already spoiled me rotten. Any more would be too much.'

But Amir simply smiled and dropped a kiss on the top of her head.

'I promised you the affair of a lifetime,' he murmured against her hair. 'And that is what I intend to deliver. But not just yet.'

Briefly he glanced at his watch, nodding approval at what he saw.

'For now, it's still Easter,' he said huskily, turning her naked body in the bed so that she faced him once more, cupping the warm, silken weight of her breasts in both hands. 'Still spring. And you know what they say a man's mind turns to in spring.'

'Yours turns to that at any time!' Lydia retorted, her breath catching in her throat as he lifted her breasts to meet the heated demand of his mouth.

'Mmm,' Amir murmured against her skin, his breath feathering over the sensitivity of one tightened nipple, making her shiver in delicious anticipation. 'Spring and summer and autumn and winter…'

His tongue flicked out, encircled the aching bud, then he drew it softly into his mouth and suckled hard. And with a yearning cry of surrender, Lydia gave herself up to his lovemaking once again.

CHAPTER TEN

AT AROUND three in the morning Lydia finally gave up on
any hope of falling asleep and slipped soundlessly from
the bed. Leaving Amir deep in apparently dreamless oblivion, she tiptoed from the room and downstairs to the living
room, pulling on her ivory silk robe as she went.

By rights, she too should have fallen asleep as easily as
Amir, she reflected as she curled up beside the still-
glowing embers of the fire he had lit earlier. But just as
she had always done on special occasions as a child, she
had found herself unable to relax, still too keyed up by the
excitement and delight of the day.

And what a day it had been! There had been so many
wonderful moments, so much to enjoy, making her feel as
if she were fizzing inside, her blood actually sparkling in
her veins. She had no longer seemed to be living in the
real world, but as if she had been transported to some
fantasy existence where every day was a holiday and she
had only to wish for something for it to be granted her.

She had still been recovering from Amir's ardent lovemaking when he had slid from the bed and pulled on his
jeans, snatching up his mobile phone and barking enquiries
into it in incomprehensible Arabic. Obviously the answers
had pleased him because he had been smiling in deep satisfaction when he had come back to the bed to rouse her
from the half-sleep into which she had drifted.

'Come on, *habibti*,' he urged, shaking her gently. 'Time
to wake up—we're going on holiday.'

That jolted her awake in a second.

'We're *what*? Amir…we can't!'

'We can. It's on the list. Number—'

'No, don't tell me, I remember. Number nineteen. Going on holiday. Sun, sea and sand. But this is London in the middle of a snowstorm in February. *How…?*'

'You'll see. Just come with me—trust me.'

Trust him! Lydia felt that if he had asked for her life she would have given it into his hands in the perfect confidence that he would take care of her and make sure that everything went right.

If there was a way to produce sun, sea and sand, then Amir would do it. She had no doubt of that.

But all the same she was stunned when the chauffeur-driven car took them to one of the largest, most luxurious gyms in the area. To a place where the swimming pool was not just the usual, clinically blue-tiled rectangle but an artificial idyllic beach in miniature, complete with sand, palm trees, and a special wave machine to make sure that the temperately heated water lapped against their feet in gentle movement.

Sunbeds reproduced the 'sun' part of the holiday, and Amir had even thought to provide a perfect, azure-blue bikini that he had ordered from the boutique they had visited the day before. To Lydia's amazement and delight, it not only fitted perfectly but also flattered and enhanced her figure wonderfully.

The mirror told her half the story on that, but the rest of it was there in Amir's eyes when he looked at her. In the flames of desire he didn't even try to conceal, the smouldering glance that sizzled all the way from the top of her shining bronze head, right down to the bare toes that curled on the water-splashed sand.

'As soon as I saw that, I knew it would be perfect for you,' he told her huskily. 'What I never guessed was just *how* perfect.'

And Lydia was only able to nod, her own voice having deserted her. She had been quite unprepared for the sight of Amir's sleek, bronze body as he emerged, dripping wet from the swimming pool as she appeared. With his black hair slicked back severely, every muscle toned and hard, the water drops sparkling against the darkness of his skin, he was pure Bedouin chieftain, powerful and untamed.

'In my country, water is like riches,' he told her, taking her hand and drawing her with him into the pool. 'Come with me, *habibti*, and let me bathe you in this most precious of elements. We have only the briefest of summers together, let's not waste a moment of it.'

The 'summer' Amir gave her lasted only a couple of hours, and she knew that, even as a child when she had wept at leaving the places where she had spent such a magical time, she had never packed away her bikini with so heavy a heart.

It wasn't just the end of the holiday he had created for her; it was the knowledge that with each hour that passed now, the length of their time together was diminishing fast. Already their second day would soon be over. So as she joined Amir in the luxurious limousine that was to take them back to his apartment her eyes burned with tears she did not dare to shed.

'Do we *have* to leave?' She sighed.

'Even the most wonderful holiday must come to an end, sweetheart.'

Amir had caught the betraying sheen in her eyes and he took her hand with an understanding that tore at her heart.

'But perhaps this will help lighten your spirits. Happy second anniversary, Lydia.'

'This' was a small, beautifully wrapped package that he produced from a pocket and slipped into her hand. Opening it, Lydia found that it contained a pair of the most beautiful diamond earrings.

'Oh, Amir!'

The gift was spectacular, the earrings exquisite, but what choked her up the most, tearing at her heart with bittersweet delight, was the realisation that once again he had remembered and marked the exact minute that they had met.

'Amir, they are *beautiful*. I really don't know how to thank you!'

'Don't you?'

His voice had deepened, grown husky, and the arm that lay lightly around her waist tightened, drawing her closer, his head coming down as he took her lips in a searing kiss of promise.

'I think you know only too well how you can thank me,' he murmured against her mouth. 'We both know.'

The rich, deep voice matched his kiss in a pledge of passion, the hungry demand in the lips that took hers making heat flood through her body so that she shifted restlessly against him, already aching with the hunger only he could appease. Once again, the journey back to Amir's apartment was going to be a long, long purgatory of waiting and anticipation.

'Yes,' she sighed, and it was a sound of surrender and delight in the same second. 'Yes. I know.'

She had thought—had hoped—that as soon as they reached the house he would take her straight to bed, but she was wrong. Instead, as soon as she entered the apartment, she stood stock-still, staring around her in stunned delight.

While they had been out, it seemed as if an army of skilled, industrious elves had been busy transforming the whole of the hallway and the living room beyond into a Christmas wonderland. An enormous tree, festooned with twinkling lights and baubles in silver and gold, stood in the corner, multicoloured parcels piled up at its feet. Beautiful garlands swathed the wooden banisters, the walls, the windows. Candles burned everywhere and even a bulging stocking hung from the wide mantelpiece of the huge fireplace.

'Happy Christmas, sweetheart,' Amir murmured in her

ear, but this time she could find no words to thank him. She was only able to stand transfixed, her hands up to her face, covering her mouth, tears of sheer delight tumbling down her cheeks.

And that hadn't been an end to it, Lydia recalled now, pulling the robe tighter round her and curling up on the edge of the hearth, hugging her knees, staring into the dying embers.

Somehow Amir had also provided a choir of carol singers, children with voices so beautiful they had brought tears to her eyes. Jamila had cooked and served a traditional dinner with all the trimmings. And, of course, the snow, still coming down in gentle flurries outside, had provided the perfect, Christmas card touch of beauty.

And then there had been the presents. A wonderful mixture of the wildly extravagant generosity she had come to expect from this man together with small, inexpensive gifts. But gifts that had been chosen with such understanding, such knowledge of her that they had made her head reel. They had only been together for a short while, but in that time Amir had listened and learned and his presents proved that he knew her almost as well as he knew himself.

But like the 'holiday' that afternoon, 'Christmas' could only last a few hours. They had made the magic stretch just a moment or two longer by staying up till midnight and toasting an imaginary New Year in vintage champagne. After that, Amir had made love to her right here, on the thick soft rug before the fire, his touch, his kisses, the final wild conflagration of her orgasm the perfect end to the perfect day.

But even the perfect day couldn't last for ever.

Lydia sighed, reaching for a log from the nearby basket and tossing it on the fire, watching as the flames flared suddenly and began licking greedily at its edges.

For ever was the one thing Amir could not provide.

The one thing he had no intention of providing.

For ever was not in Amir's vocabulary.

And that was why she was sitting here like this, unable to sleep.

A wave of misery swept over her, clouding her eyes, and the cheek that she laid against her silk-covered knees was once more damp with tears. But these were not the tears of joy she had shed earlier, or the sobs of ecstasy that had escaped her at the height of the lovemaking before this hearth. They were tears of desolation and regret at the thought that most of the three days that had seemed to stretch ahead so wonderfully, filled with all sorts of possibilities, were now in the past. Her time with Amir was almost over and she didn't know how she was going to face the future without him.

'Lydia...'

The soft sound of Amir's voice startled her, bringing her head up sharply, wide blue eyes going to the door. As always, her heart jolted wildly at the sight of him. Even with his black hair tousled, dark eyes still faintly blurred by sleep and the stubble of a daylong growth of beard shadowing his strong jaw, he was easily the most lethally attractive man she had ever seen.

'I'm sorry! Did I disturb you? I tried to leave as quietly as possible.'

'It wasn't anything you did. I was only sleeping lightly anyway.'

Well, it was half the truth, Amir told himself. He *had* found it hard to lose himself in the oblivion of sleep. But the real fact of the matter was that he had missed her. It had only taken a couple of seconds for the emptiness on her side of the bed to register, to penetrate the light doze into which he had drifted. She had barely closed the door behind her before he had been wide awake, staring at the ceiling.

At first he had fully intended to stay where he was and

wait for her to come back. She would only be a minute or two, he'd reasoned, and when she returned he could pretend that her getting back into bed had woken him. It would be the perfect excuse to put his arms round her, draw her close. They could make love again in the still, dark silence of the night. Already his body had been growing hard just at the thought.

But Lydia hadn't come back. And lying awake in the dark room had given him too much time to think. Because of the blackness, the stillness, he'd seemed so much more aware of everything, from the cooling space where Lydia's slender body had been to the faint ticking of the clock on the bedside table. That sound was suddenly too loud, too intrusive, reminding him of the way that time was ticking away, and with it this brief idyll of an affair with Lydia.

All too soon she would be gone, flying to America and that wonderful new job of hers.

And how would he feel then?

Suddenly too restless to stay still, he had flung back the bedclothes, pulling on a pair of black pyjama trousers and a matching silk robe, belting it tightly round his lean waist against the chill of the night as he went in search of Lydia.

'Couldn't you sleep?'

She shook her bright head, the tumbled waves flying round her face, and he had to struggle to control the instinctive kick of response low down in his body that made him want her all over again.

'No. Too much excitement for one day. My grandma always said it wasn't good for me. "There will be tears before bedtime," she would tell my mother.'

'My grandmother used to say much the same thing.'

Amir came and sat on the couch near her, holding out his hands to the fire.

'Did she? But I thought…'

'My English grandmother—on my mother's side. I

never knew my father's mother. Would you like something to drink—some tea perhaps?'

Once again Lydia shook her head and this time the immediate response was harder to take as he caught the faint, sweet scent of her hair and her body.

'What I'd like to do is to talk.'

'Talk? About what? Anything in particular?'

'About you.'

Lydia knew her mistake as soon as she had spoken. She saw his dark head go back, the swift narrowing of his eyes. His long, relaxed body tensed up immediately, rejection of what she had said stamped into every inch.

A couple of days before, his reaction would have silenced her, making her fear his possible response, the angry rejection of her enquiry that might follow. But now she had little or nothing to lose. They only had one more day together. And she couldn't leave knowing so little about him, knowing that he had never really given her anything of himself.

'Play fair, Amir!' she protested. 'You asked me enough about myself. You know about my job, my family, my friends. Now it's my turn.'

Talking wasn't what was on his mind right now. The fire had caught more strongly, the flames flaring round the log, lighting the darkness of the room. The golden flickers came and went, creating subtle patterns on her upturned face, gilding her skin and turning her hair to molten bronze. His imagination was throwing wild, heated ideas at him. Images of laying her down on the thick rug before the fire, stripping the delicate silk of the robe from her even softer body and making hot, passionate love to her while the light of the fire played over her naked flesh.

But a second look at her face told him that even to try it would be the wrong move. And perhaps she was right.

Talking would slow things down, increase the anticipation, prolong the pleasure of simply being with her, knowing what was to come. The wild, heated pleasure of the first twenty-four hours had been amazing. Mind-blowing. The best sex he'd ever had. But he had also come to find a whole new sort of delight in the quieter moments. In simply sitting beside the water of the swimming pool, combing the tangles out of her hair, or joining in the 'New Year' ceremony she had insisted on following.

'We have to write down the things of the past year we want to put behind us and burn them up in the flames of a special candle,' she'd said. 'We record the good stuff as well, but that we put into an envelope and keep it for the coming year.'

And as he'd assumed that for the sake of this invented New Year, the 'past year' she'd referred to had simply been the time since they'd met, that had been easy to do. The one thing he'd had to regret was that they hadn't met earlier. Another day, another time, when he could have spent longer with her, getting to know her own unique individuality, enjoying more of the white-hot passion that blazed between them.

But perhaps it was better this way. At least, with the restrictions of the three days that was all the time they had together, there was no chance of the gloss ever fading, reality setting in—or, even worse, boredom.

So, 'Okay,' he said now. 'What do you want to know?'

Lydia couldn't believe her luck. Where she had expected an outright refusal, it was almost shocking that this had been so easy. Looking into his eyes in the light of the fire, she had seen the flare of a sensuality hotter than even the physical flames and had felt an immediate, answering shiver of response. If he had turned on his lethal, irre-sistible, seductive charm, she would have been lost. Unable to resist him, she would have responded at once, and this moment would have been lost.

But something had changed Amir's mood, and, terrified

of altering the atmosphere again, she hunted for a safe topic on which to begin.

'Tell me about the horses you breed.'

That was easy. Within a moment he was launched into describing the stud, the stallions he owned, the race winners he had bred. From there it was an easy step to his childhood on his uncle's farm, growing up as an English boy to all intents and purposes, but always knowing that there was something different about him.

'When did you find out the truth—that Sheikh Khalid was your father?'

'On my eleventh birthday.'

Amir turned his head to stare into the fire, the leaping golden flames reflected in miniature in his onyx eyes.

'My father had arranged a visit to a stud a couple of miles away, owned by the father of a friend of mine. As it was in the summer holidays, I was there, helping with the horses. I led out one of the stallions he was interested in. But it was me that he stared at; me that he watched. I never realised before then just how much I looked like my mother.'

Moving abruptly, he leaned forward to pick up another log and toss it deep into the heart of the fire.

'When I told her all about it, she decided that perhaps the time had come for me to know the truth.'

Lydia bit her lip hard, imagining how that must have felt. Reacting instinctively, she moved to sit closer to Amir, curled at his feet. When she laid a sympathetic hand on the hard curve of his knee he dropped his own to rest on top of it, strong fingers curving over hers.

'From that moment I vowed that I would make my father acknowledge me for who I really was. That one day I would hear him call me his son, no matter what it took.'

The hard mouth firmed, setting into a ruthless, unyielding line, and Lydia shivered faintly inside at just the thought of that pitiless determination being set against anyone, even the proud, cold-hearted old man his father obviously was.

'And I was even more determined when I visited Kuimar, first as a tourist and later to negotiate deals, to buy and sell the horses I bred—to watch them race. It quickly became my true home—as if I had never been away.'

Amir's broad shoulders lifted and fell in a resigned shrug of acceptance, jet-black eyes not leaving the fire, as if he was seeing in the wood and the flames the image of the country of his birth.

'I fell in love with the place and spent as much time as I could there. It's a country of such contrasts. The cities that are a dazzle of glass and chrome, and the wind-blown sand-dunes that are never the same shape from one day to the next. To the east there are the Hajar Mountains, to the west, the waters of the Gulf itself. I learned to love both the bustle of the city life and the still, eerie silence of the desert at night.'

'It sounds wonderful.'

Her soft murmur drew those brilliant eyes to her face, so that she saw the shadows of memory that still lingered in their depths.

'It is,' he said simply.

Kuimar is my country. The words she had heard him speak—was it truly less than twenty-four hours ago?—echoed inside Lydia's thoughts, making her wince inwardly in hidden pain. Had it really been only that morning that she had first heard him make the declaration that she knew spelled the death sentence for any foolish hopes she might have had of a future beyond the three days he had allotted her?

She might have been able to fight his past, or even the fact that he didn't love her—yet. But how did she fight a *country*?

'So that's why you only have three days? Because you're expected back in Kuimar—at your father's side?'

He took so long in answering her that she knew there was more to it than that, and her heart quailed inside her at the thought.

What more could there be? More than the fact that he was a Crown Prince and his father's heir. More than the fact that his heart belonged to his country.

'That's part of it,' he said at last.

'Only part? So what's the rest of it?'

Oh, *why* did she have to ask? Why couldn't she just keep quiet and leave it alone? Her time with him was almost up as it was. Did she truly want to complicate it now, with things that soon wouldn't matter?

Soon she would be gone and so would he. They would be thousands of miles apart, flying in opposite directions, going to different corners of the world. Soon his reasons for returning to Kuimar would be irrelevant because he would have gone and she would never see him again.

Today, she had the terrible suspicion that those reasons might just ruin what little was left of her three-day affair.

And still Amir was silent, looking down into her waiting face, his expression impenetrable as the face of a marble statue.

'Amir?' she prompted hesitantly, knowing that she had to have an answer and yet dreading the moment when he would actually say the words.

His deep sigh was even more worrying than his silence. Her heart clenched in fear as he raked both his hands through the darkness of his hair, ruffling it even more.

'Don't, Lydia,' he said, the softness of his voice doing nothing to calm her fears.

'Don't what?'

In contrast, her own tone was wild and sharp, revealing the turmoil of emotions she was struggling with.

'Don't ask? Why not? Is it something so dreadful?'

Her voice died on a small choking sound as he laid a finger over her mouth, silencing her.

'Can't we leave it as it is?'

She almost gave in to him. Almost nodded in agreement. Almost said yes, fine, they could leave it unsaid, she didn't want to know.

But she couldn't. Because she *did* want to know. Whatever it was.

And so with a movement that tore at her heart she pulled away from that gently restraining finger and shook her head firmly.

'No. We can't leave it.'

'Lydia…'

His sigh destroyed what was left of her self-control, shattering her ability to stay calm and wait.

'Amir! *Tell me!* Tell me now.'

'All right.'

His tone was heavy, lifeless.

'You asked. I have to return to Kuimar to get married. My bride is waiting for me there.'

CHAPTER ELEVEN

IT HAD been one of the longest nights of her life.

If Lydia had thought earlier that she would find it difficult to sleep, now she found it impossible. She lay there in bed, staring at the ceiling, seeing nothing, and all the time in her head Amir's words repeated over and over.

'I have to return to Kuimar to get married. My bride is waiting for me there.'

If anyone had told her that the man she had fallen head over heels in love with was going to say those words to her, and asked her to predict her reaction, she would have thought that she would scream or shout, certainly that she would cry out. She might have thought that she would slap him, or at least pummel her fists against his shoulders, demanding to know what he was doing, why he was treating her in this appalling way.

She had done none of those.

Instead, pride had come to her aid, giving her at least an outward dignity that her inner soul didn't possess. Inwardly she was screaming and weeping with the best of them, but her outward appearance revealed nothing of her distress.

She was proud of the way that she hadn't even uttered a sound. That she had got slowly to her feet, her head high, chin lifted defiantly. She had even managed to look Amir straight in the face with a strength she hadn't known she possessed. That strength had kept the tears away too, leaving her totally dry-eyed in spite of the knowledge that a torrent of weeping was building up against the dam inside her heart.

'And when were you going to tell me this?' she asked,

her voice as stiff and cold as her tightly held body. 'At the end of the three days? As you waved me off at the airport?'

'Never.'

The single word almost destroyed her. Blindly she reached out for the back of a nearby chair and held onto it with a desperate grip that turned her fingers white against the gold upholstery.

'Never?'

The ebony eyes were totally expressionless, blank and opaque.

'It wasn't relevant to our relationship.'

'Relevant!'

A mixture of fury and pain made her spell out every single syllable of the word coldly and precisely.

'You don't think that the fact that you're engaged, that you're getting *married* to someone else has anything to do with us!'

Big mistake, Lydia! You know there *is* no 'us'! That even Amir's use of the word 'relationship' was just politeness. He told you from the start that three days were all you'd have. Deep down, you know that the reality is that emotionally this means as little to him as that one-night stand you thought you were at the start. It just happened to stretch out a bit longer, that's all.

And if she'd needed any confirmation of that fact, then Amir's cold, tight smile as he got to his feet gave her it in spades.

'My relationship to my future wife is strictly between her and me. It has no bearing on this situation at all.'

'Except in that she is why you only have three days to spare to dally with me? I take it that you would have flown out to her two days ago, if the snow hadn't got in your way?'

'That is where I was going.'

Cold and clipped and curt, his words were like a death

sentence to any foolish hopes she might have harboured that she'd got it wrong.

'And, yes, if the snow hadn't closed the runways, I would have been in Kuimar by now.'

'And happily married and off enjoying your honeymoon somewhere in one of Daddy's better palaces, no doubt!'

'Not exactly. A royal wedding is a weeklong affair.'

Amir wished he could find a way to handle this situation better, but his mind seemed to have gone totally blank. All he could think of was how white and still she had gone, how darkly bruised her eyes seemed, deep as pansies above ashen cheeks.

She hadn't actually stepped away from him, but her withdrawal was as total as if a huge, impassable chasm had just opened up between them, yawning at his feet. If he made the wrong move she would turn and run and he would lose her for ever.

He wanted to reach out and enfold her in his arms, to kiss away that frozen look and tell her that it was not as it seemed, not as she thought, but the time wasn't right for that. Not yet. So instead he stuck to telling her the strict truth, even if it seemed to make matters worse for the moment.

'The ceremony wouldn't have been performed yet.'

'Oh, I'm glad to know that!'

Lydia didn't recognise her own voice in the one that spat venom into Amir's impassive face, savage bitterness hiding the agony that clawed at her heart.

'I'm glad to know that you wouldn't actually be being *unfaithful* to your fiancée just yet! I'm sure that must salve your conscience—absolve you completely.'

'Lydia, don't be bloody stupid!'

Amir's hands flew up and out in a gesture of total exasperation.

'I'm not looking for absolution! It's not relevant...'

'You're very fond of that word!'

'It's the most appropriate one I can think of!' As always his accent deepened and darkened with his rising temper.

'And was it because it wasn't *relevant* that you never mentioned this small matter of the fiancée you had? The wife-to-be who was just waiting for the ceremony to be performed.'

'I never lied to you.'

'No, you never *lied*! You just omitted a few vital facts. Didn't you think it would have been more honest to tell me everything? To give me all the details so that I could make an informed choice?'

'You knew where you stood from the start.'

'Oh, yes, I knew where I stood!'

And where she stood was precisely nowhere. She had just been a passing fancy to him. Someone with whom to while away the unexpected interval of waiting for his flight out to Kuimar and his wedding. And she had fallen straight into his honeyed trap.

Amir's dark head lowered so that he was looking straight into her ashen face. His eyes were brilliant and cold, devastating in their complete withdrawal from her.

'You knew exactly what the situation was. I told you I could offer you no more than three days. And you accepted. You went in with your eyes wide open.'

But he hadn't told her the whole truth! And that being so, she had foolishly, naively, *idiotically* let herself hope that, given time, she might change the situation for the better. She had actually allowed herself to believe that she could change his mind, win him round to loving her.

She couldn't have been more wrong.

He had no love to give her. He was already committed to another woman.

She had to get out of here. She couldn't stay in the room a moment longer. Not long ago, she had watched his stunning, expressive features in the firelight and known that she loved him. Now she didn't know if she loved him or hated him. She only knew that she couldn't look into his dark, handsome face and maintain any degree of composure. If she didn't escape she would break down completely and risk telling him exactly how she felt about him.

'I'm going to bed,' she said through lips that seemed to have been formed out of ice, they were so stiff and cold and awkward. *'Alone,'* she added pointedly when he nodded and half turned towards the door.

She would break completely if he so much as suggested that he came with her. If he touched her or tried to kiss her, then she would disintegrate into a shaking heap of despair, crumbling at his feet. As it was, she barely felt that her legs would support her on even the short walk to the door.

But Amir said nothing, made no move. He simply nodded and the rush of relief at the thought that he was going to let her go without a fight gave her an unexpected renewal of strength.

'I'm going to—to *my* room,' she managed, though the words almost stuck in her throat. 'You said that I could be totally private there. I trust you will respect that.'

'Of course.'

If his face had been carved from marble, his eyes as sightless as a classical statue, he couldn't have looked more distant from her. It was impossible not to contrast his expression now with the way he had looked at the time when he had made her that promise, on the second night she had spent in this apartment.

'I wondered if you were free tonight?' he had said when he'd phoned her up. 'If you'd like to do something—a meal—a film maybe.' And in a rare moment of reality in this whole fantasy affair, they had done just that.

After they had made love on their return from the shops, they had lain together for a long time, just holding each other. Then eventually they had got up, showered, dressed, and gone out. They had seen the latest Hollywood blockbuster, sitting in the back row, cuddling and kissing like teenagers, and then gone on to a restaurant for a meal.

Arriving back at the apartment, decidedly more high on atmosphere, pleasure, and the sheer intoxicating force of Amir's personality than on the couple of glasses of wine she had drunk, Lydia had consulted the 'sensual stages' magazine article and turned to him with a mock petulant pout.

'I'm supposed to be able to invite you in for coffee, but it can't be done. I don't have anywhere to invite you to! This whole apartment is yours. There's nowhere that's mine alone.'

That was when he had taken her by the hand and led her up the stairs. On the large, wide landing, he had turned in the opposite direction to his bedroom, finally stopping outside a door at the far end of the corridor.

'Here,' he had said, flinging it open to reveal a huge elegant room, beautifully furnished in soft shades of gold and cream. 'This is yours.'

It was more than a room, Lydia discovered. It was a whole suite, with a luxurious bathroom, a dressing room where the clothes he had bought her had already been un-packed and hung up, and a small sitting room on one side.

'This is your private space for as long as you are here. I promise you I won't come in here. I won't even cross the threshold, unless you give me permission. It's yours and yours alone to do with as you please.'

And then, while she had still been staring in delight and disbelief, he had come closer, cupping her face in one hand as he'd turned her face to his.

'So now…' he had whispered huskily, ebony eyes burning down into her darkened ones, telling her forcefully without the need of words just what was in his thoughts '…invite me in.'

Of course, apart from that one night, she'd never used the room as her own. She'd never needed to—until now.

But tonight the thought of somewhere private, some personal sanctuary that she could run to and hide, was like a haven from the torment of being with Amir and knowing how he had deceived her. Blinded by stinging tears, Lydia blundered up the stairs and along the corridor, diving into 'her' suite like a small, terrified animal seeking refuge from a ruthless predator.

Slamming the door shut, she fell back against it, holding it closed as if afraid that in spite of his promise Amir might still come after her, still demand that she let him in.

But of course he didn't. And even though just a few moments later she heard the heavy sound of his footsteps on the stairs and tensed, it soon became clear that he had turned in the opposite direction, heading for his own room.

And it was only then, as she sank down on the edge of the bed, and let her misery wash over her, that Lydia finally gave way to the despair that was in her heart.

It had been one of the longest nights of his life, Amir told himself as he headed down the landing to Lydia's room later that morning. He had hardly slept at all. Instead, he had lain awake for hours, knowing he'd made a pig's ear of everything, and trying to think of a way to sort things out.

There was only one way, of course. And that was to tell the whole story and then let Lydia make up her mind what happened from then on.

And that was the really terrifying bit. The putting everything into Lydia's hands and waiting for her to decide. He'd never let any woman have that much power in his life before. If he was honest, he'd never let any woman have *any* power in his life at all. He'd run things his own way, and that had always suited him.

So what had made things so different? he asked himself as he rapped sharply on the panels of the firmly closed door. He couldn't begin to explain. He only knew that when he'd seen her walk away from him last night, it had been the hardest thing he'd ever done to let her go. Harder even than accepting any of the rejections his father had handed out to him. But he'd also known that, right then, going after her had *not* been the thing to do. She hadn't been ready for it, and it could only have made matters worse.

And all the hours he'd spent in the big double bed, lying awake in the darkness, the thing he'd been conscious of was the space beside him. The cold emptiness of the sheets where Lydia's warm, softly scented body should have been. It seemed impossible that after only a couple of days she should have made such an impression on him, and yet, dammit, he'd *missed* her.

'Lydia? Are you awake?'

Silence.

Perhaps she was still asleep.

No, that explanation didn't convince. The memory of her white, miserable face swam before his eyes and he knew, without having been told, that there was no way that the woman who had left him last night would have been able to sleep, any more than he had.

She had to be awake, but not responding to his call.

'Lydia! We have to talk.'

Still no response. But then he knew she was stubborn as a mule.

A faint smile touched his mouth as he recalled the way she'd blanked him at first. The struggle he'd had to even get her to let him sit down, let alone talk to her. He'd had to work hard to win her round, even to the point of making it look as if he'd been about to walk away…

Not that he could have done it.

The smile became rueful as he shook his head in despair at his own foolishness. Even then he had been so totally under her spell that he hadn't known what he'd been doing. From the moment she had walked into the lounge at the airport he had been trapped, entranced, caught up in her spell and unable to break free. Even if he *had* walked away, he knew he would have had to go back. She had got to him so badly that his mind, his actions hadn't been his own.

They still weren't.

'*Lydia!* I know you're listening. Open this damn door, will you?'

This was crazy. If he had any sense at all, he'd leave it right here. It would be for the best all round.

All he had to do was to walk away, and things could go back to how they had been. How they had been three days ago, before he'd first set eyes on her. Then he'd had his life all planned out, totally clear-cut and defined. He'd known exactly where he'd been going. What had been going to happen to him. And then Lydia's appearance had turned everything upside down, thrown his plans into chaos.

He hadn't thought beyond that first night. But when he'd learned that the airport was closed for the next couple of days, he'd grabbed at the chance to spend more time with her because by then she'd really got under his skin, and there had been nothing he'd been able to do about it. But three days was all he'd said. And those three days were almost up.

'Okay, forget it! I know you're awake; I know you're listening. But if you don't want to talk, then that's up to you. I'm going downstairs to make some coffee… If you want to join me, fine. If not…'

If not, then this time he wasn't turning back. This time he'd walk away without a second glance. If she wanted to end it now, then that suited him. He'd have his life back under control and it would be as if this uncharacteristically crazy, irrational interval had never been.

And that suited him fine.

So why did he find himself filling two mugs with coffee? And heating the milk to add to one, just as Lydia liked it?

He was just going to try and get her to see sense, he told himself as he headed for the stairs again. Just going to get her to talk…

His foot was on the first step when the phone in the hall rang, loud and shrill.

Lydia heard the phone from behind the security of her locked door. The sound of Amir's voice didn't reach her, but she knew from the way that the faint buzzing sound stopped that he had answered it almost at once. Which meant that he was not going to come back—not yet at least.

But he would come back at some point, she was sure of that. He had sounded so cold, so ruthlessly determined when she had heard his voice on the other side of the door, that she knew he didn't intend to give in without a real fight.

'We have to talk', he had said, and she knew that, inevitably, at some point they would have to. But she couldn't face him, didn't know what to say to him. And so she had hidden away behind the locked door taking the refuge of silence, when all the time every sense had been on red alert to even the faintest sound he made.

He would be coming back any minute. With the phone call answered, he would be heading back upstairs. She couldn't stay holed up in this room all day long.

But as she waited the time ticked by, seconds turning into minutes, and still there was no sign of Amir, no sound of movement from outside.

Was he coming back? Or was she just deceiving herself that it even mattered to him? Perhaps he'd given up on her completely? After all, the three days were almost up. Would he really think that the final few hours were worth all the effort of fighting for?

Eventually she couldn't bear the waiting any longer. It

was obvious that, whatever Amir was doing, he wasn't coming back. And as she couldn't stay in her room for ever, she would have to face him some time, sooner rather than later. Hastily she dressed in her own clothes, the ones she had arrived in. She didn't feel she could wear anything that Amir had bought her.

'Amir?'

The silence in the house was oppressive as she came down the stairs, looked in all the rooms.

'Amir? Are you there?'

No answer. Had he gone out, then? Certainly the weather looked clearer, heavy rain turning the snow to slush very quickly.

So what did she do now? What could she do but wait? But first she'd make herself a cup of coffee. Perhaps with something warm inside her she'd feel stronger.

Somehow without Amir's presence the kitchen seemed to have lost some of the cosy friendliness of before. On the table lay the magazine Lydia had brought with her and as she waited for the kettle to boil she flicked through the pages desultorily, skimming the sections she hadn't looked at before. Suddenly a familiar face in a photograph caught her eye and she froze, staring down at it.

'Eligible royal bachelors' read the heading to the article and there was a picture of Amir, tall and proud, raven head windswept and tousled, mounted on a magnificent Arab stallion. The article enthused in decidedly breathless prose:

> Sheikh Amir bin Khalid Al Zaman might have been brought up and educated in England, but at heart this gorgeous Crown Prince is truly a magnificent son of the desert.

Lydia could barely read any more through the burning tears that filled her eyes, blurring her vision so that she had to blink hard to drive them back. Only brief sentences here and there caught her attention, and all of them were guaranteed to add to her already bitter discomfort.

'Love 'em and leave 'em seems to be his philosophy when it comes to women. No single female, however lovely, has ever caught his heart and held it for more than a few blissful months... But when the break-up comes, this Prince of Kuimar knows how to sweeten the pill with a vengeance. Every one of his former lovers has been sent on her way with a jewel or two worth something close to a king's ransom. Not enough to mend a broken heart perhaps, but very nice just the same.

'Sweeten the pill, indeed!'
Unable to take any more, Lydia tossed the magazine away from her, careless of the fact that it slid along the polished surface of the table and tumbled onto the floor.

The idea of the coffee no longer appealed and instead she made her way out into the hall, where she lingered at the doorway into the living room.

All trace of the Christmas decorations had been cleared away, the magical atmosphere disappearing with them.

'Face facts, Lydia,' she told herself aloud. 'There never was any magic there in the first place. It was all a delusion.'

As she spoke the sound of the phone rang out again, cutting into her words. Automatically Lydia moved forward to answer it, then stilled again as the answer machine clicked on.

On the table beside the telephone were the two pages torn from the magazine—was it really only two days before?—and she stared down at them, missing the beginning of the message.

'You asked us to let you know when flights were leaving again,' the disembodied voice spoke onto the tape. 'The runways are just about clear now, and we hope to get back to a normal service very soon...'

So that was it, Lydia reflected unhappily. The three days were over, even sooner than Amir had anticipated. The time she had spent here, with him, had come to a close.

The message clicked off but she was hardly aware of the silence. Slowly she ran her finger down the page, seeing how so many of the stages had been checked off, completed, done.

'First date, coffee...' she whispered, picking stages out at random, remembering bitterly. 'First kiss... Going to bed together...'

'Some of them we've rather jumped the gun on.' From nowhere, Amir's words slid into her mind, stabbing at her painfully. It was no wonder that he had grabbed at his opportunity. He must have thought that she was easy, cheap. He'd had only to click his fingers and she had jumped to do as he'd wanted.

But not any more. Now it was all over. Wincing as she recalled her own naïve enthusiasm, Amir's bemused reaction, Lydia saw that almost all of the stages detailed in the article had been ticked off.

'I promised you the affair of a lifetime.' Once more an echo of his voice tormented her. *The affair of a lifetime.* Oh, yes, he'd given her that all right. For a second she allowed herself to remember how it had been yesterday, the magic of every moment. But now nearly all the necessary stages were behind them. There were only the final few left on the list. Just number twenty-four and...

Twenty-four.

'The cost is a pittance and you'll need it for number twenty-four.'

He'd said that to her in the dress shop. She could still remember the saleslady's widened eyes, the look of shock on her face.

What *was* number twenty-four? Picking up the page, she turned it over, looking for the item she was seeking.

'Stage Twenty-four—he takes you somewhere really special. The best restaurant in town, or a really funky club. Perhaps he has an extra-special proposal in mind?'

'Never!' Lydia found herself saying out loud.

'Or perhaps this is his way of letting you down gently.'

But by moving the magazine page, she had disturbed something else. A note, she realised, her heart clenching on a thud of shock. It could only be from Amir; the firm, confident scrawl could be no one else's.

'Lydia,
Called away unavoidably. Sorry—but it really is important. I know I promised you three full days, and now I can't deliver. But I'll be back tonight and then I'll make it up to you. We'll go out—anywhere you want. Wear the blue dress, the one I bought for just this occasion, and we'll make the last dinner of this three-day affair one you'll remember for ever.

He hadn't even bothered to sign it, she thought miserably. He hadn't needed to. No one else but Amir would simply issue a decree like that and expect her to obey it.

'Wear the blue dress...and we'll make the last dinner of this three-day affair one you'll remember...'

'Oh, Amir!'

She didn't know if what she was feeling was agony or fury. She only knew that it felt as if her heart was shattering into tiny, irreparable pieces, splintering away inside her. His name was a moan of pain on her lips and she folded her arms tight around her body, trying desperately to hold herself together.

It was as she spun away from the table that she saw it. A large box, coloured in a soft turquoise with elegant black lettering on the top. The name of one of the most expensive and exclusive jewellers in London.

'But when the break-up comes, this Prince of Kuimar knows how to sweeten the pill.' The words of the article she had read just moments before came back to haunt her with a terrible bitterness. 'Every one of his former lovers has been sent on her way with a jewel or two worth something close to a king's ransom.'

'We'll make the last dinner of this three-day affair one you'll remember for ever.'

Was she really going to wait around for Amir to come back just so that he could take her out, say goodbye properly, maybe even take her to bed one last time—and then give her her jewelled handshake?

Once she might have dreamed that given time he could have come to love her, but now she saw her dream for the delusion it truly was. Tonight their affair was to come to an end, he would reward her for services rendered, and then he would walk away without so much as a backward glance.

No!

She had more pride than that.

The airport had said that the runways were clearing. If she was lucky she could get on a plane and be gone before Amir even came back.

She'd take the initiative from him. It was the only thing she could do for herself now, the only way she could preserve some dignity. Better to cut off the relationship hard and sharp than drag out goodbyes until they became unendurable.

Picking up a pen and pulling a second piece of paper towards her, she reached for the phone.

CHAPTER TWELVE

'MISS ASHTON, the manager would like to speak with you in his office. Immediately.'

Lydia's nerves tightened on a twist of apprehension as she turned and headed in the right direction, crossing the ornately tiled floor of the hotel foyer.

She supposed that one day, eventually, she would be able to respond to a summons like this without some such reaction. That she would be able to settle into her new job without constantly looking over her shoulder and worrying and wondering if Amir was going to appear. But not for a long while yet.

She didn't know what malign fate had meant that the very first posting she had received from Halgrave had been here, in Hafit, the capital of Kuimar; she only knew that she wished it could have been anywhere else. But because it *was* her first post, there was no way she could turn it down, though she'd tried to fight against it, and so, desperately unwillingly, she had now been living and working in Kuimar for three days.

'Come!'

The voice that greeted her knock on the door was muffled by the wood and no sixth sense alerted her. But as soon as she stepped into the room and saw the tall, upright figure standing by the window she suddenly knew that she was in very deep trouble.

He was standing with his back to her, and the fact that he was wearing the traditional Arab robes, together with the white *gutra* headdress bound with a black and gold cord or *igal* meant that she couldn't see his face, or even his colouring. But she didn't need to see. Every instinct

149

had immediately gone straight onto red alert, telling her just who was in the room with her.

'*Amir!*'

He turned slowly. So slowly that it seemed as if her heart had time to stop beating entirely, only to start up again in a thudding, uneven pulse as they finally came face to face.

It seemed impossible that she could have forgotten the impact of that imposing height, those stunning features. That just over six weeks' absence could have blurred the edges of her memory and dimmed the brilliance of those polished obsidian eyes, the hard, high line of the forceful cheekbones, the beautiful bronze tones of his skin.

She would have said that time had been merciful in helping her that way, except that now it meant she was subjected all over again to the stunning realisation of just how beautiful he was. And, after all this time without it, just the sight of him was like a draught of the coolest, clearest water to someone dying of thirst in the desert, an indulgence for which all her senses clamoured loudly and hungrily.

'Good afternoon, Ms Ashton.'

The greeting was accompanied by a faint inclination of his head, too slight to be anything but condescending, too condescending to be anything other than sarcastic. The sleek suited businessman, the casually dressed Amir she had seen so briefly in London had totally disappeared. Here, in his native land, he was a Bedouin ruler from his head to his feet.

'What a pleasure it is to see you again.'

It was a struggle to keep his voice even, Amir admitted. His mind seemed to be splitting in two, one half delighting in the sight of her again, the other flooded with dark anger at the memory of the way she had left without a word. He didn't know if the throbbing pulse at his temple was in response to the sensual appeal of that lovely face and the long, slim lines of her body in the smart navy-blue dress that modestly covered her arms and her knees in respect of local convention, or a bitter fury that threatened to break out of control.

'I have missed you.'

He laced the words with enough acid to make her wince visibly, though she covered it up hastily.

'I'm sorry I can't say the same about seeing you!' Lydia flashed back. 'Quite frankly, I would have been much happier if I'd never set eyes on you again. I never wanted to come to Kuimar. It was the last place on earth I would have chosen to work, if I'd had the choice—but of course I didn't.'

'No, you didn't.'

Something in Amir's voice, the faint smile that flickered on his beautiful mouth and then off again, tugged sharply at Lydia's nerves.

'And what, precisely, does that mean?'

Suspicion sharpened her tone, sparked in the blue depths of her eyes, earning her a swift, reproving frown.

'My dear Lydia, I was simply agreeing with you that the choice was not yours to make.'

'And whose precisely was it?' she questioned edgily, struggling to ignore the cruel edge to that 'my dear Lydia'.

'Why, mine, of course.'

This time, his smile was pure malice, turning her blood from heated anger to cold discomfort in the space of an uncertain heartbeat.

'Yours! And what did you have to do with it?'

Once more that calculated smile was switched on and then off again, never once touching his eyes, which remained as cold and hard as jet.

'Kuimar is not a country that welcomes single European women to its workforce. Before filling the position in this particular hotel, the manager and the directors of the Halgrave Group had to submit a list of possible candidates from which I, as Crown Prince, made my selection. Knowing it was the company you worked for, I suggested that your name was on that list. Then, naturally, I chose you as the most suitable applicant.'

'Naturally,' Lydia echoed hollowly. Then suddenly she shook her head sharply. 'No, it's not *natural* at all! I can see no reason on earth why you should want to have me here in your country after what there was between us! I would have thought that you were far more likely to be glad to see the back of me and never want the two of us to come face to face again.'

'You couldn't be more wrong.'

Lydia was coming to detest that smile. If a deadly cobra could be capable of smiling in the moments before it struck, then that was exactly the sort of expression it would assume. It was both hateful and dangerous, a threat and a warning all rolled into one, and with nothing pleasant about it at all. And it made a sensation like the slow, creeping slither of something icily nasty slide uncomfortably down her spine just to see it.

'Since your unexpected departure from London six weeks ago, I would have moved heaven and earth to find you again.'

'You would? But why?'

'We have unfinished business between us. A three-day affair that lasted only three quarters of its time. Promises that weren't kept. Certain *stages* that were not worked through.'

'I think we accomplished all the vital ones. No?' Lydia queried as Amir shook his dark head slowly.

'No,' he stated, harshly unyielding.

'What did you want—*blood*?'

'Not blood, my darling. Something much more vital than that. Our affair did not end the way I wanted it to.'

'Well, tough!'

Lydia marched up to the big polished wood desk that

dominated the office and glared at him fiercely across it. He'd got every damn thing he'd wanted out of that affair. He'd had his fun with her, then tossed her aside in favour of the poor, betrayed bride who had been waiting for him here in Kuimar.

'It ended the way *I* wanted it. I'm perfectly happy with the way things turned out.'

Liar! her conscience reproached her bitterly.

If you were perfectly happy you wouldn't have wept into your pillow so many nights since then. And your heart wouldn't have ached just at the mention of Kuimar and its Crown Prince. And if you had wanted the affair to end then you wouldn't have spent every day since you knew you were coming to this hotel in the dread of just such a meeting as this, knowing it must be inevitable.

'But I'm not happy,' Amir declared coldly. 'And I intend to rectify that. I had plans for that last night.'

'Oh, I'll just bet you did! And I suppose you thought that I'd go along with them, no matter what! Well, I'll tell you this, Your High and Mightiness! I do have some moral standards, and one of them is that I don't have affairs with married men.'

'I am not a married man.'

'Near as dammit! It may not matter to you, but in my book an engagement is well on its way to being as binding as a wedding. I don't believe in being unfaithful to any-one...'

'Neither do I,' Amir inserted smoothly, stopping her dead.

'But—but you were going back to Kuimar, to your bride. You were getting married. You're married now!'

She choked her words off again as Amir held up long, elegant hands, spreading them so that it was only too evident that there was no ring on any of his fingers.

'And is that supposed to convince me?'

Desperately she tried for scorn to hide the way that cruel

acid was eating away at her heart. Now, when she was least able to cope with it, when it was the last thing on earth she wanted to remember, her mind would keep throwing at her the memory of how it had felt to have those strong yet gentle hands on her skin, the pleasure they could arouse with just a touch. Every secret, hidden pleasure spot on her tingled into wakefulness and wanting as something primitive and potent called from Amir's body to her own.

'Credit me with a little intelligence, Amir! It would be the easiest thing in the world to take off your wedding ring, leave it at home!'

'Then if I swear it on my honour, will you believe me?'

Lydia flung a fulminating glare into his dark, cold face.

'Do you think for one minute that I believe you have any honour to swear on?'

'I'm not married, Lydia. I have no plans to be married in the near future. I'm not even engaged to anyone.'

He *sounded* sincere. It terrified her how easily she was tempted to believe he *was* sincere. But it was a risk she dared not take.

'I don't believe you!'

'Believe it!' he insisted harshly. 'Because it's the truth. I *am not married*. Nor am I likely to be married unless things change very dramatically.'

'But—what happened?'

Black eyes locked with blue, making her fear that he could read her thoughts and see in her face the sudden, irrepressible flare of delight at knowing that he was still free that would not be held back, no matter how she tried.

'You happened,' he stated flatly.

That floored her.

'Me? I… How could I…?'

'The marriage was part of my father's plan for me. It was to be an arranged marriage. He had picked out a bride for me. A bride of perfect character and breeding for her role as my wife and the future Queen of Kuimar. I had never met her.'

She shouldn't be feeling relieved. She *shouldn't*!

None of this meant that he had cared any more for *her*. It wouldn't have changed a thing about their relationship. But just knowing that this unknown bride had not been his choice, that she had not been the bride of his heart, eased something of the cruel nagging ache that had been her constant waking companion, ever since the night Amir had told her about his impending marriage.

'I didn't even know her name.'

'And yet you would have *married* her?'

'Why not?'

His shrug dismissed her question as totally irrelevant.

'You didn't love her!'

'I'm Arab enough to feel that the western emphasis on love was heavily over rated. I'd never been in love with someone strongly enough to want to commit my life to them. Never met anyone I couldn't just walk away from in the end, so this was no great sacrifice to me.'

Well, that put her squarely in her place! 'Never met anyone I couldn't just walk away from in the end.' She had known that anyway, but somehow it hurt so much more to hear him actually speak the words, to see the coldness of his eyes as he looked at her.

'Love doesn't come into an arranged marriage.'

He had to get her off this uncomfortable line of questioning. He was beginning to feel as if he had been edged into a corner, with his back very firmly up against the wall. They were heading into territory where none of the beliefs he had had about himself held true any longer. But he didn't know yet just what he could put in their place.

'If the couple is lucky, that may come with time, but it isn't a prerequisite of a successful union.'

'But—what was it you said—character and breeding is?'

'Character and breeding and my father's approval.'

'Oh, of course!'

She'd forgotten about that. Forgotten the one thing that gave his bride an advantage above and beyond all others. That she could help him win the thing he wanted most out of life—the kingdom he believed was his birthright from his father.

'Except that none of those matter now because the marriage isn't going to take place.'

'You haven't explained why.'

Don't let yourself hope, she warned her vulnerable heart silently. Don't even *dream* that it could have been because of me.

'Why?'

Amir reached into a pocket, pulled out a piece of paper and tossed it at her, watching stony-eyed as it fluttered down onto the polished top of the desk.

'That's why.'

Lydia stared in shocked consternation at the newspaper picture of herself and Amir, taken on their first day in London, when they had paused for a meal during the shopping expedition. Their heads were close together and she was smiling straight into his eyes.

And anyone but a fool could have seen the way she felt about him, she told herself on a shiver of apprehension.

'Who took that?'

'Some reporter with nothing better to do. They don't matter. What matters is that Aisha saw it. My father saw it. The wedding was called off.'

And he was *furious* about it. It glittered in the depths of his ebony eyes, drew every muscle in his handsome face tight over his amazing bone structure.

'Which is why you are here.'

'Me?'

Lydia's pulse started to throb a warning, and instinctively she took an unsteady step backwards away from the danger signals she could see in his eyes.

'I'm here to work!'

'Do you really think I went to the trouble of ensuring that you came here just so that you could manage an hotel?'

'It's what I'm trained for! What I want to do!'

'I have other plans for you!'

She didn't like the sound of 'other plans'. And when had he moved? She hadn't noticed him coming towards her, prowling across the thick rug with the silent pace of a hunting cat. And yet suddenly he was in front of her, reaching out to still her when she would have turned away.

'You have no right to have any plans for me whatsoever! You've no part in my life...'

Her voice cracked, croaked, died completely as she saw the way he shook his dark head.

'I have every right. You see, my father believed he was getting not just a son, but a dynasty. Heirs to his throne. That's why he arranged this marriage. The marriage that has now been called off—because of you.'

'Because of *you*!' Lydia tossed back, her chin coming up, blue eyes blazing defiantly. 'You seduced me!'

'We seduced each other, sweetheart,' Amir drawled, injecting silky menace into his tone. 'And this picture proves it.'

There was no denying that, Lydia admitted miserably, looking again at the photograph and at the hands linked on the top of the table, the total concentration of the man on the woman and vice versa, the heads so close they were almost touching.

'My father still wants those heirs. He wants grandchildren.'

Lydia's head flew up again, her eyes widening as the full impact of his words hit home with a vengeance.

'You can't mean...'

'I want to give my father the heirs he craves. To do that, I have to have a bride. Because of you, the bride who was chosen for me is no longer prepared to marry me. The only solution that I can see is that you should take her place.'

'Oh, no! No, no, *no*! No way! You can't do this to me! You can't make me!'

'I am Crown Prince, heir to the throne.' The declaration was pure arrogance, undiluted by even the tiniest touch of hesitancy or conscience. 'I can do as I please.'

'You still can't force me! I didn't come here for you, I only came because of my work. I just want to get on with my job.'

'In order to work in this hotel you will need the permission of a member of the royal family.'

'In other words, you? Then I'll find another job—any job!'

'In order to do *that* you will need the permission of the royal family.'

'Then I'll resign—go home…'

Once more she caught the dangerous glint in his eyes.

'No, don't say it! To do that I will need the permission of a member of the royal family! That can't be true! There would be an international incident if you kept me here!'

'Do you really think that you are that important?' Amir scorned. 'Besides, how would anyone know?'

'I'd phone the embassy—or…'

That hateful, cobra's smile was back, totally destroying what little was left of her shattered composure.

'You can't do this, you know!' she tried again in desperation. 'All I have to do is to go to the airport, get on a plane—any plane going to anywhere…'

'No plane can take off or land at the airport or fly anywhere without the permission of a member of the royal house. It is not a law that we usually trouble much about enforcing…'

'But in this case you'll make an exception,' Lydia finished drearily, knowing that she was staring defeat right in the face. 'But this is barbaric. You can't force me into a marriage I don't want.'

'Your tongue says you don't want it...' Amir murmured softly.

Reaching out one long hand, he trailed the backs of his fingers softly down her cheek, watching intently as, in spite of herself, her eyelids drooped in languid delight at the gentle caress.

'But does your body agree?'

'Yes...' Lydia tried to begin, but he had moved faster than her thoughts and the word was crushed by his lips, the sound of it smothered into a sigh. And in the tiny space between one breath and another she knew she was lost.

Her head was swimming, her pulse beat wildly. She couldn't get enough of his kisses and she knew that with every movement of her body, with the small, moaning cries that escaped her, she was encouraging him to kiss her harder, caress her more. His hands roamed urgently over her, sparking off tiny infernos wherever they touched, and her own fingers tugged at the unfamiliar lines of his robes, seeking some way of reaching the intimate warmth of his skin.

When she couldn't find that, she laced her hands tightly in the raven strands of his hair, pulling his head down to hers to deepen and prolong the kiss. And all the time she was hotly, hungrily aware of the thick, potent force of his arousal pressed into the cradle of her hips.

'Enough!'

With an abruptness that tore at her body and soul, Amir wrenched up his head and put her from him, long hands gentling her, holding her upright as she swayed unsteadily on her feet.

'This is not the place for this. When I take you to my bed again, I want the privacy of my own room, not to provide a public spectacle in one of Kuimar's best hotels.'

When, Lydia noted ruefully. Not *if*. He was totally sure

of his conquest of her. And who could blame him? She hadn't even tried to protest, to assume a pretence of modesty or reluctance. And there was no point in trying to do so now. She wouldn't be convincing anyone, least of all herself.

'You're very sure of yourself,' she managed, her voice shaking weakly.

Amir looked down into her clouded eyes and smiled.

'No, *habibti*,' he murmured softly. 'I am sure of *you*.'

'I haven't said yes yet!'

'Perhaps not.'

He shrugged off her protest with supreme indifference. 'But you will.'

She didn't even dare to think how right he was for fear that he might read it in her face. Could she really turn down a chance to be married to this man she loved so desperately even if he didn't love her?

'And it would be worth the sacrifice, would it? In order to get this kingdom of yours and your father's approval? You'd tie yourself in marriage to a woman you don't love?'

'I was prepared to do it once. I will happily do it again.'

If only she knew, Amir thought. If only she realised *how* happily he would do it. And for reasons that had nothing whatsoever to do with the kingdom or his father.

For the past six weeks he had felt as if he were only half alive. He had lost all his zest for life, his interest in anything. But not now. Now after just an hour in her company his whole body was buzzing with a feeling like an electrical charge and he felt more animated, more awake, than ever before.

'And when the woman involved is as beautiful, as desirable as you are, then it will be no sacrifice at all. To keep you with me, by my side in the daytime, and in my bed at night, I would sell my soul to the devil himself.'

If she hadn't been looking down at the newspaper pic-

ture as he spoke, then Amir's words might not hav
quite the same impact. But Lydia had just glanced c
as he spoke, her gaze drifting to the revealing photogra

Just moments before, she had been horrified at what
had revealed about her feelings for Amir, but now, sud
denly, she was seeing it in a very different light. The couple in the picture were like mirror images in the way their
heads were inclined towards each other, hands linked. And
although Amir had his back to the camera and so his face
could not be seen, it was evident that both pairs of eyes
were intently locked together.

*To keep you with me... I would sell my soul to the devil
himself.*

Was it possible? Or was she just deceiving herself? Was
she letting fantasy take control of her mind so that she was
seeing things that she wanted to see?

'So,' Amir said harshly. 'What is your answer?'

If he really wanted her in any other way than his hard-
hearted declaration had made clear, then he was doing a
wonderful job at hiding it. But perhaps he was the one
who was hiding?

And how would she ever know if she didn't take a
chance to find out?

'My answer?' she said carefully, exerting every ounce
of control she possessed over her voice so that it didn't
give away just how important this was to her. 'My answer
is this. When we met in London, you promised me three
days and the nights that went with them. You promised
me the affair of a lifetime. You still owe me that.'

Something in that arrogant, ruthless face had changed.
The onyx eyes were suddenly hooded and a muscle
worked in the stubborn jaw. But did that mean that she
was right in her hopes—or that she couldn't possibly be
more wrong? Either way, her whole future could depend
on what happened.

'I'll take those three days all over again, Amir. But this

we'll have them here, in your country. Show me
mar. Show me why you believe it's worth selling your
for. And when the three days are over, then I'll give
u your answer.'

CHAPTER THIRTEEN

ONCE again Lydia had three days.

But this time she didn't need the full seventy-two hours. This time she knew from the start what her answer would be. She knew exactly how she felt. She just didn't know what was in Amir's mind.

And that was the most important thing of all.

Because she had always known that she didn't need three days to make up her mind. She had known what her answer to Amir was going to be in the first second that he had made his intentions plain, and there was no going back.

She was so deeply in love with him that there wasn't even a question to answer. He was as essential to her life as the air she breathed, the blood pulsing in her veins. The weeks they had been apart had taught her that she could no longer live without him, no matter what it cost her to live with him.

And by the end of the first day after her declaration, she knew she was also falling in love with Kuimar as well as its prince.

In the hotel, where most of the duplex suites even had their own *en suite* swimming pools, she had already had a taste of some of the luxury available, but now she encountered some of the real sights, sounds and smells of Amir's birthplace.

'I'll never need to wear perfume again!' she exclaimed when they were alone on the evening of the first day, a day she had spent meeting the female members of his family. 'My clothes are saturated with the scent of that aromatic wood they burned. What was it you called it?'

...h.'

...ir smiled, lazily watching her as she put her nose to ...leeve and inhaled appreciatively. He hadn't been able ...ook away from her all day. She was like some brilliant, ...oriously coloured butterfly, drawing and holding his gaze with every movement, every gesture, every laugh. And when he had thought he would never hear it again, the sound of her voice was like the flow of gentle water in his ears, washing away the confusion of the past and filling up the empty spaces inside him.

'It's burned as a sign of welcome. Obviously, it would originally have been used in a tent, to perfume it ready for the arrival of a guest, and at women's parties every guest would waft the smoke over her head or settle over the burner to allow the scent to permeate her clothing.'

'Presumably taking care not to set herself on fire!'

'If you think the air was perfumed tonight, you wait till you visit the spice *souk*. There the whole market is drenched with the scent of cinnamon, frankincense and dried roses. I'll take you there tomorrow.'

'And I want to see the gold *souk*—and the silks...'

'You don't have to visit the markets for those.'

Amir stretched out on the huge, luxurious bed and clasped his hands behind his head, leaning back against them.

'I can have anything you want brought to the palace.'

He wanted to give her everything she desired. Everything she'd ever dreamed of. If she let him, he would fulfil every fantasy she had and some she'd never even begun to think about.

If she would let him. That was the real problem. He had resorted to threats and bluster, behaved like a primitive Neanderthal to keep her here, but could he maintain the pretence? Could he really hold her captive, imprison this beautiful creature, just for his own happiness? To do so

would mean breaking her bright spirit and he k
could never forgive himself if he did that.

But she had promised him three days. And when h
thought that she had gone out of his life for good, e
three days seemed like an eternity. He was determined
put them to good use, try every trick in the book.

'You only have to say. As my wife…'

'I'm not your wife yet, Amir!

His indolent self-assurance set Lydia's teeth on edge.

'I haven't said yes! I haven't even given you any sort
of an answer.'

And he hadn't given any indication of the way he was
feeling. Oh, he had been unfailingly attentive, indulgent
and good-humoured all day. But if he felt anything deeper
he had shown no sign of it.

'I could still say no.'

Try it, those glittering black eyes warned, sending a
shiver down her spine. Just try it and see where it gets
you.

'You could,' Amir said slowly. 'But after today would
you want to?'

'After today?' Lydia questioned, deliberately misunder-
standing. 'Oh, you mean now that I have seen the palace—
the luxury you live in? Now that I've walked on marble
floors, had my way lit by spectacular chandeliers, bathed
in a bathroom where all the fitments are made out of gold.
You think that I would marry you for *that*?'

'Many women would. I've met enough of them.'

'Then I'm not one of many women. Don't you think
that if the money was what mattered to me, then I'd have
made sure I took all the clothes—everything you bought
me—when I left the first time?'

She'd hit a wrong note there, bringing a dark frown to
his handsome face. Clearly he'd taken it as an insult that
she had rejected his gifts, leaving them behind when she
had gone to America.

. them all flown out to you here.'

.ould never admit to her how he had felt, the sense
..s that had hit him like a blow when he had opened
.oor to 'her' room in the London apartment and seen
her clothes still hanging in the wardrobes. Her perfume
.ad lingered on the air as well, tugging at his memory,
naunting him for days. He had spent more hours than he
cared to remember sitting in that room, in the darkness,
just breathing in her scent.

'So you did, but clothes won't influence my decision.
You forget, Amir, I'm not happy with the idea of an arranged marriage. I told myself I would only ever marry
for love. To me, a marriage without feeling would be as
dry and arid as the desert out there beyond the mountains.
It would be empty and barren and all the wealth in the
world couldn't turn it into a temperate oasis where flowers
and trees would grow.'

He was trying completely the wrong approach, Amir
told himself. It was time he changed tack swiftly.

'Don't you like the idea of being a queen one day?'

If she could be queen of his heart, it would be a different
matter. That was the only place she wanted to reign.

'I really hadn't thought about it,' she said honestly.

'Well, think about it!' Amir growled. 'Think about being Queen of this country and mother of the heirs to the
throne—'

'Which reminds me,' Lydia broke in impulsively.
'When do I get to meet your father?'

Now what had she said to put that scowl on his face?

'My father has gone to his palace in the mountains for
a few days. Perhaps when he returns...'

'Perhaps!'

Lydia's blue eyes flashed with an indignation to match
the anger in her tone as she swung round to face him.

'Perhaps! What is this, Amir, do you not think I'm fit
to meet your father?'

'Don't be foolish!' Amir tossed back at her. 'A prospective bride, you are fit to meet with anyone. It's that…'

Just that if King Khalid met Lydia now, before he h her promise to marry him, then the old man would surer let slip the truth about the marriage to Aisha and the reasons why it had fallen through.

'Just that…?'

She had to blink in astonishment as she saw the way that his frown suddenly disappeared, swept away by a smile of such deliberate brilliance, such sensual provocation that it made her toes curl into the softness of the rug.

'Just that for now I want you all to myself.'

One hand lifted, curved into an imperiously beckoning gesture.

'Come here,' he said and the lordly, arrogant tone grated on her raw nerves, stripping away a protective layer of skin so that she stiffened in instinctive rejection.

'Please…' he added very gently, his eyes softening, seeming to plead with her. And immediately all her resistance melted with a speed that made her sag weakly like a puppet whose strings were cut so that it fell in a limp heap on the ground.

Somehow Amir had sensed her reaction because, even as she thought she might fall, suddenly he was there beside her, the strength of his arms coming round her, supporting her, bringing her gently down to the bed to lie beside him.

'You are wrong about the desert, *habibti*,' he murmured, pressing warm lips against her cheek, trailing kisses down her throat to the point were her pulse beat at the base of her neck. 'It may be dry and barren, but it is not empty or dead. And it can be very, very beautiful.'

His tone soothed her, held her still, as his hands smoothed the dress from her shoulders, slid it down her body.

'The dunes can be as smooth and rounded as the curves

flesh, and every bit as warm,' he murmured, strok-
hand along the long line from shoulder to waist,
up over the arc of her hips. 'Or they can be wild and
ospitable, blown into tortured shapes by the wind.'

Leaving her dressed in only the briefest scraps of silk
and lace, he turned his attention to her hair, pinned up into
a neat chignon because of the heat. Long hands gently
eased out the pins, then combed softly through the bright
strands, massaging her scalp with his fingertips while all
the time his lips kissed her into a state of mindless oblivion.

'You are too tense, sweetheart,' he said suddenly, and
she heard the frown in his voice rather than saw it on his
face.

'Too much coffee,' Lydia offered, trying to make light
of the matter.

She didn't want him to suspect that the real reason for
her tension was his presence. That inside a private little
war was raging between her gloriously aroused senses and
the strict demands of self-preservation.

One side had already half yielded to his caress, the
heavy, honeyed ache of desire starting up between her legs.
The other side warned despairingly that to give in to
Amir's lovemaking now would only leave her far too vulnerable in the future. How could she ever hope to say no
to marriage if she said yes now?

'You should have warned me that the way to show I'd
had enough to drink was to turn my cup upside down.'

The finger she had lifted to his face to administer a small
tap of reproach refused to obey her, gentling instead and
turning into a slow caress down the lean plane of one
cheek.

'And as for the *halva* and those pastries! I swear I can
still taste the sugar on my lips now.'

Teasingly she let her finger run over his mouth, tracing
the firm outline of his lips.

'There's even some still here on yours,' she to.
looking deep into his eyes.

The flare of hunger she saw there told her everyt
she needed to know. Unexpectedly for Amir he lay ba
his head cushioned on the downy pillow.

'Kiss it away for me,' he murmured lazily, sensual hunger thickening his voice.

Lydia slid over the silk covers until she was half lying
on top of him, supported by the hard wall of his chest.
With deliberate slowness she brushed her mouth against
his, lingering softly, letting her tongue slide out and follow
the same path as her fingers. Under her caress she heard
Amir's low sigh of surrender and she angled her head more
so as to deepen the kiss.

Her senses had won, she realised hazily as heat flooded
her body. They had swamped any sort of rational thought,
drowning it out completely with the throbbing pulse of
sexual hunger.

Only then did she become aware that Amir had not been
lying submissive as she'd thought. While she had concentrated on his kisses, he had removed the final slivers of her
clothing, replacing them with the heat and strength of his
hands. And now he shrugged off his own clothing, coming
back to her proudly naked and fiercely, powerfully
aroused.

Lydia gave a small, shaken gasp as he pulled her towards him, then lifted her bodily until she was straddling
him while he lay on his back, the hard, hot strength of him
probing the centre of her femininity. Looking down into
his hard-boned face, she saw the blaze of colour along the
carved cheekbones, the shimmer of desire in his eyes.

'Never fear the desert, darling,' he told her roughly.
'Not when I am with you. The sands may shift and swirl
until you can't see where you're going, but I'll take care
of you. I'll make sure I'll always keep you safe.'

She had opened her mouth to answer him, only to find

words would come out. There was nothing in her
...ts but the need for his possession, the longing to
...him deep inside her, filling her completely.

...he no longer cared about self-preservation or the wis-
...m or lack of it in what she was about to do. She had
...ever really planned to say no to Amir's demand for marriage. To do so would be like cutting out her own heart
and throwing it on a fire. She couldn't live without Amir,
and even such a loveless marriage as he proposed—on his
side at least—would be better than nothing.

'Promise?' she managed, her voice raw with the need
she couldn't hide from him as he stroked her intimately,
with devastating effect.

'On my life,' he assured her harshly, shifting slightly so
that he could thrust up and into the innermost core of her;
a shaken gasp escaping him as he felt her tight muscles
close about him.

And as she took him into her, abandoning herself to the
burning pleasure his passion triggered all over her body,
Lydia told herself that it would be enough. He might not
love her, but he wanted her. And for now that was enough.

CHAPTER FOURTEEN

HE'D waited long enough, Amir decided. At least, he waited as long as he could bear.

Okay, so technically the three days weren't yet up. They still had one more night. Eight, ten more hours before Lydia had promised to give him her answer.

But he couldn't stand not knowing.

He couldn't endure one more sleepless night lying beside her, hearing the gentle sound of her breath, inhaling the scent of her skin, feeling her soft, slender body curved against his, and wondering if she planned to stay or go.

Because if she decided to go then he knew that he wouldn't be able to stop her. For all his attempts to intimidate her, his threats to force her into staying, he knew now that he could never carry them out. Even as he had made them he had known that they were just so much empty air, forced out of him by sheer panic and desperation. The knowledge that, having found her again, he couldn't let her go.

And if he had felt that way then, now it was all so much worse.

Because now, at last he had admitted to himself just what she meant to him. And by doing so he had acknowledged that if she went she would take his whole world with him.

He had to know now what her answer was. He'd waited long enough.

'Move over...'

She looked up at him in astonishment, her eyes widening slightly at his tone, the hard set to his jaw. And that was hardly surprising. Only a few minutes before, they had

171

...ing a shower and putting the heated enclosed
...more sensual use than simply getting clean.

...vhat had brought about this change of mood? Lydia
...ered as she shifted position on the couch, giving him
...n to sit beside her. What had happened to the relaxed,
...iling Amir of just seconds ago?

'I know now why you love this country so much,' she
said in an attempt to distract him from whatever unwel-
come thoughts had darkened his mind. 'I've never seen
anything as spectacular as the desert in the moonlight, or
heard anything as eerie as the sound of the wind amongst
the dunes.'

She tried to smile as she spoke, the warmth fading rap-
idly from her face as she met with a stony, flint-eyed response. Without a word, he took from her hand the comb
that she had been using to smooth the tangles from her
freshly washed hair and began to ease it through the shining bronze swathe.

'Mmm, that's *good*...'

She let her head fall back, giving herself into his hands,
enjoying the gentle tugging sensation. If she left it, surely
he would tell her what was wrong in his own good time.
Making him feel pressured was certain to make him clam
up even more.

'I think— Oh!'

She broke off on a cry of surprise as, abruptly as he had
picked it up, Amir tossed aside the comb and pulled her
back until she was lying almost in his lap, her head supported by his strength, long, still-damp tendrils of hair
spread out over his arm. The only place to look was up
into his dark, handsome face, and what she saw there set
her nerves painfully on edge.

'What's wrong?' she began hesitantly. 'What...?'

'What's wrong?' he echoed so harshly that she winced
as if the words had actually been cruel blows falling onto

the delicacy of her exposed skin. 'I'll tell you wrong—*we're* wrong. You and me.'

'You and me,' Lydia echoed shakily. 'What—*why* we wrong?'

Had he completely rethought his plans? Had the secon three days been just long enough to make him change his mind? Had he decided that he no longer wanted to marry her?

'Because we're neither one thing nor the other! We're not having an affair, nor are we doing anything else.'

'And what would you want us to do?'

'You know what I want! I want you to marry me.'

'To be your princess and one day your queen?'

His only response was a brusque nod, his black eyes opaque and unreadable. If that was the only reason she had for staying, he wasn't going to argue. Just so long as she stayed he didn't care *why*.

'To give your father the heirs he wants? To win you his approval and make you truly the Crown Prince of this country?'

'Yes, dammit. Yes! For that, for anything, for whatever else you want! Lydia, I can't wait any longer. I need you to tell me. I need to know what your answer is.'

'My answer...'

She didn't know why she hesitated. She only knew she suddenly couldn't get the words out.

She had known that this moment would come. That at some point she would have to give him his answer, and she had fully resolved just what that answer would be. She knew he didn't love her. She also knew she could cope with that. She could cope with anything if he only stayed with her. If she could only be his wife.

So why could she not say it now?

'Lydia...'

His low, raw-toned use of her name was a warning not to try his patience too far. He had already risked his fa-

...isapproval because the marriage to Aisha had been off, and he was not prepared to do so again. To win the old king's affection, he needed a wife, and he ...nded that that wife would be her.

'Never fear the desert, darling.' The words Amir had ...poken barely two days before came back to haunt her now. 'Not when I am with you. The sands may shift and swirl until you can't see where you're going, but I'll take care of you. I'll make sure I'll always keep you safe.'

In her mind she had a vision of the desert as they had ridden through it only that evening, the brilliance of the stars glittering against the night-dark sky. The dunes had been a vast and silent void and looking at them she had suddenly known what true emptiness must be like. Without Amir, her life would be as desolate as that, but with him, knowing that he could never love her, wouldn't she know another desperate form of loneliness?

'I'll always keep you safe,' he had said. But this hurt was one thing he couldn't protect her from. Because he didn't even know it existed. And just the thought of that terrible emptiness made her shiver deep inside.

'My answer...' she tried again, fighting the stab of anguish that made her voice quaver. 'My answer is yes.'

'*No!*'

She couldn't believe what she'd heard. He couldn't have said it, could he? Had he...?

'Amir?'

But he was already hoisting her up into a sitting position, getting to his feet. Striding away from her, his long straight back taut with rejection.

'Amir? What is it? Please look at me.'

She saw the muscles in his shoulders tighten, but even then she wasn't prepared for the white, drawn expression on his face when he whirled round to face her, the blaze of rejection in his eyes.

'Amir, I—I said yes.'

'And I said no. I've changed my mind, Lydia. I do want this. I never wanted this.'

'I don't understand—what are you trying to say?'

'I'm not trying to say anything! I can't make it any clearer. It's over! Finished! I don't want to marry you.'

At least, not like this. He had been a fool to think that he could cope with this. That he could take so little when he needed so much. He had hoped that she felt something for him, even if it was only the white-hot desire that burned them both up when they touched. But now it seemed that even that had gone.

He could have taken anything. But not that look of fear in her eyes.

When she had looked at him like that something had died deep inside him. He felt as if his heart had shrivelled into ashes, crumbling away.

There was no way he could keep her with him if she felt like that. No way he could look at her every day and not see that moment of panic, no matter how bright the smile, how cheerful an expression she tried to hide behind.

The thing he had most feared was breaking her spirit and now it seemed that he had come desperately, dangerously near to doing just that.

'Amir?'

He couldn't meet her eyes for fear that she would see how close he was to breaking too. But he couldn't let his feelings show now. The one thing, the only thing he could do for her was to set her free as soon as possible. But if he looked into her face then it would destroy him completely. And so he stared at a point in the distance, deliberately not focusing on anything.

'The whole idea was a mistake. A stupid one on my part. I thought I could still have everything, but now I see that I don't want it after all.'

'I don't want it after all.' Could he have said anything

re cruel, anything more savagely hurtful, more guar-
teed to destroy her totally? 'I don't want to marry you.'
I don't want you.

If he had ripped out her tongue by the roots, he couldn't
have done more to make sure that she didn't argue or
protest. Every single word had died in her throat, her
tongue froze in her mouth. She could only stand silently
and watch as he suddenly leapt into action.

A tug on a bell-pull summoned servants. A few brusque,
barked commands sent them scurrying to do his bidding.
A click of his fingers, and a mobile phone was brought
and a stream of unintelligible Arabic poured into it. Only
when they were finally alone again did he draw breath and
turn his head in her direction.

'It's all arranged. You can leave tonight.'

'Tonight!'

Lydia shook her head in dazed disbelief. This couldn't
be happening. Only moments before, she had been ready
to answer his proposal of marriage, anticipating the prospect of spending the rest of her life with him. But now he
had turned that hope of a future upside down.

He couldn't wait to get her out of his life, it seemed.

'But I can't—I haven't...'

'Your bags are being packed as we speak. A car will be
here for you in ten minutes. The jet will be waiting for
you at the airport. It will leave as soon as you are safely
on board.'

'So this is goodbye?'

What else could she say? A tiny, desperate voice at the
back of her mind was shrieking at her to protest, to argue,
to fight her case, but even as she opened her mouth to do
so she knew that even to try was futile.

'Yes. Goodbye. Have a safe journey.'

His eyes were as bleak and dead as his voice. He might
be looking at her, but she was sure that he didn't *see* her
in any way at all.

'Amir, please don't do this.'

It was a last-ditch attempt. Short of going down on he knees and pleading with him not to do it, she couldn' think of any way to get through to him. Perhaps if she had been able to cry, if he could see desolate tears pouring down her cheeks, then he might understand just how terrible she was feeling inside. But of course now, of all times, was the moment that her eyes chose to be burningly, painfully dry, her heart breaking secretly, inwardly, without any sign on the outside.

'I don't want to go.'

'And I don't want you to stay.'

He couldn't take much more. If she had to go then he wanted her to leave *now*, straight away. He couldn't cope with standing around, making stilted, awkward conversation as if she were just some passing acquaintance, someone he'd shared a few pleasant hours with, and not the woman with whom he had wanted to share the rest of his life.

In fact he couldn't bear to see her walk away.

'There's no point in dragging this out. I never was one for long drawn-out goodbyes. Far better to make it short and sweet and have it done with.'

Short and *sweet*!

He actually held his hand out and expected her to take it. She couldn't touch him. If she did she knew that the flimsy barriers that were all that were holding her emotions in check would splinter totally, letting the flood tide of anguish and misery pour through. And she would never be able to pick up the pieces.

Far better to keep her dignity now and at least walk out with her head held high.

'Goodbye, Amir,' she said stiffly, ignoring the proffered hand. 'I wish I could say it's been nice knowing you.'

At least she had the satisfaction of seeing him wince at that. But if she had got through to him then, a moment

er he had covered it up, his emotional armour back in
ace.

'I hope your father won't be too disappointed about the
grandchildren.'

Amir's smile was brief, hard, and totally emotionless,
no trace of light in his eyes at all.

'Oh, I'm sure my father will understand. In fact, he'll
probably have another bride lined up for me within the
month.'

'Then I hope you'll be very happy together.'

If she opened her mouth again, she feared she might
actually be sick. Her pain was choking her, gathering in a
tight, bitter knot at her throat, cutting off the air so that
she had to gasp for breath.

Luckily at that moment one of the servants that Amir
had sent off to carry out his orders appeared in the doorway to be greeted by a swift, curt question.

Evidently his answer was the one Amir had been waiting for because he nodded, snapped a dismissal, and turned
to Lydia.

'Your car is here; Kahmal will take you to it. The driver
knows where to go. If there's anything you need on the
plane, you only have to ask.'

He had turned on his heel and was gone before she even
had time to register that she too had been dismissed, striding away from her and out of the room without so much
as a backward glance.

Left alone, Lydia could do nothing but turn and follow
the servant who led her out into the enormous hall where,
amazingly, her bags were already waiting, and from there
to the main door of the palace where the car stood ready,
engine purring. The sound of a clock striking behind her
stunned her with the realisation that Amir's orders had
been obeyed strictly to the letter.

The car would be here in ten minutes, he had said. And
precisely ten minutes later she was stepping into the pow-

erful vehicle, sinking down wearily onto the soft leather of the back seat.

Ten minutes exactly. That was all it had taken to shatter her dreams. Ten minutes ago she had thought she was about to marry Amir, to be with him for the rest of her days. Now, just that brief, terrible time later, she was on her way out of his life for ever, never to see him again.

The journey through the darkness was a nightmare. Lydia refused to let the tears fall and instead sat tautly, perched on the edge of the seat, her arms wrapped tightly round herself, struggling to hold back the welling pain, the burning bitterness.

At the airport she was hurried through the building and out onto the runway without even the formalities of departure. Clearly Amir's orders had made sure that nothing would stand in the way of her leaving. The plane, Lydia saw with a terrible sense of inevitability, was a private jet, with the flag of Kuimar on its side.

'In order to do *that* you will need the permission of the royal family.'

She could hear Amir's words in her head as clearly as if he had been sitting beside her. Well, it was obvious that he had given his permission this time—with a vengeance! He had clearly wanted her gone as quickly as possible.

Huddled miserably in her seat, she heard the plane's powerful engines start to throb, in a few moments she would feel the movement as they taxied towards the runway. Suddenly plagued by a desperate need to have something of Amir with her in these last few minutes in his country, she reached for her handbag.

The letter Amir had written her on the last day in London was the only thing she had kept. Even though its contents were so painful that she had never been able to bring herself to open it again until now, it was the only example of something so personal to him as his handwriting. It had been in her bag ever since.

The sound of the engines changed, the jet lumbering into movement as Lydia opened the letter for the first time since that morning in London.

'Lydia…'

The letters of her name blurred as tears threatened at last.

But as her fingers tightened on the paper the feeling had her stiffening in surprise. Looking at the letter more closely, she felt her heart jolt in shock at the sudden real- isation that there was an extra sheet, attached to and folded behind the first. A part of the note that she hadn't read.

'We'll make the last dinner of this three-day affair one you'll remember for ever,' was the last sentence on the first page. The point where she had thought it ended. But what she read now made her breath catch painfully in her throat.

But before that dinner, there's something I'd like to ask you to think about. These three days have been truly special to me, Lydia. So special that I can't imagine living the rest of my life without you in it. I have a lot to explain, I know, but I'd also like to hope that you would consider the possibility of turning this three-day affair into something permanent.

With love, Amir.

With love, Amir.

Looking back, Lydia was seeing those last terrible mo- ments with Amir all over again. Seeing the bleakness in his eyes, the emotionless set of his face. Seeing it from a very different point of view. One that translated his anger into pain, turned his coldness into a terrible, agonising re- straint.

'Wait!'

The pilot couldn't hear her but she didn't care. She w
already scrabbling with the seat belt, getting to her feet.

'Wait! Oh, please, please *wait*!'

Amir kicked open the door, strode into his room and flung
himself down in the nearest chair, not even troubling to
switch on the light. Darkness suited his mood better. It
matched the shades in his mind.

He supposed that one day, some day, eventually, he
would get used to the feeling of loss, of emptiness, but it
would take one hell of a long time. Right now he couldn't
imagine how he was even going to face the coming dawn
without her.

He had given up trying to rest hours ago, and gone out
riding on one of his favourite Arab stallions, hoping to
exhaust himself into sleep. It hadn't worked. His body
might ache with tiredness, but his mind refused to let go
of Lydia's memory.

With a groan he buried his face in his hands, but in the
same instant a faint sound on the far side of the room had
him jerking his head back up, eyes searching the darkness.

'Who's there?'

Leaping to his feet, he flicked the light on, wincing at
the sudden brightness.

'Who the hell are you?'

The woman stood between the bed and the wall. She
was tall and slender, that was as much as he could tell
because her whole body was enveloped in the all-covering
folds of the *abaya*, the traditional long black robe with
gold border embroidery that Arab women wore in public.
A black scarf was draped over her head and wrapped
around most of her face so the only things visible were
her eyes and they were deep in shadow.

'What are you doing here?'

'I came to you, Highness.'

Her voice was soft and husky, muffled by the concealing veil.

'I thought you might be lonely.'

'Lonely?'

The palace grapevine worked faster than he'd ever thought.

'Lonely. Yes, you could say that.' Desolate would be more like it. 'But if you also thought that this was your chance, then I'm sorry, you couldn't be more wrong. I'm not in the market for any sort of comfort you might be offering.'

'No?'

She had moved, was coming towards him now, her bare feet silent on the marble floor. Lydia had walked like that, with that same subtly sensual sway, her body tall and elegant.

'No!'

The word was as much to deny the memory as to answer her.

'Look, I don't mean to be rude, but would you just *go*! I'm not in the mood for female company—*any* company right now. If I tell you that the woman I love has just gone out of my life, perhaps you'll understand. And there's no way on earth that anyone could fill the hole that she's left behind.'

Beneath the flowing *abaya*, Lydia's heart kicked sharply in joy. In the moment that the light had gone on she had been shocked by the change that a couple of hours had effected on Amir's face. He looked pale and drawn, black eyes like bruises above deep shadows on his cheeks.

If she had needed any proof of the truth of his declaration, it was there for anyone to see. And what a declaration of love! No woman in her right mind could ask for more.

'But perhaps I could try.'

Amir shook his head violently.

'No…'

It trailed off into a puzzled frown.

Was he seeing things? The eyes above the folds of the veil were blue, deep, vibrant blue. And that voice…

'Who…?'

The hesitancy in his voice, the shadows in the eyes tore at Lydia's heart. It was time to put him out of his misery.

'Oh, Amir, don't you know—haven't you guessed?'

The veil was hastily unwrapped, tossed away. Amir stared, black eyes stunned.

'Lydia…' Her name was a raw, choking sound. 'You came back!'

'I couldn't leave,' she said simply. 'This is where my heart is.'

And this time there was no room for doubt. This time her smile, the light in her eyes told him that there was no fear, no uncertainty, in her reply.

His arms were open wide and she ran into them without a second thought, feeling them close around her, hold her tight, and this time she knew instinctively that he would never let her go.

'But how?' he asked eventually when the first storm of feeling had ebbed, the first snatched kisses had eased some of the emptiness in their souls. 'My men had orders…'

'Oh, Amir…'

Lydia's smile was light-hearted, teasing.

'Don't you know that no plane can take off or land without the permission of a member of the royal house? So if the Crown Prince's bride-to-be gives the order that the plane must not leave the tarmac, then—well…'

She shrugged her shoulders lightly.

'He couldn't disobey me.'

'Bride-to-be…'

Amir echoed the words with a thread of awe in his voice.

'Is that what you truly are, my love?'

'If you'll have me.'

'Have you! Darling, there is nothing I could want more in the whole world.'

'But you made me go...'

A faint echo of the pain she had felt then clouded her eyes, and Amir bent his head to kiss her again, driving away the distress with his caress.

'I did it for you. I thought that you only said you would marry me out of fear. That you could see no way out. So I gave you one.'

In spite of the pain, the distress it had caused him, he had still been prepared to set her free.

'What I was afraid of was never having your love. But loving you the way I did, I knew it was a risk I was prepared to take.'

'I thought I'd trapped you. When you told me about Jonathon, I thought that I was your rebellion, your moment of wild irresponsibility, nothing more. I knew what it felt like to need someone's love and have it withheld and you had told me you would only ever marry for love. That a marriage without feeling would be empty and barren as the desert. I couldn't tie you to that.'

'And *you* said that you'd never loved anyone strongly enough to want to commit your life to them. Never met anyone you couldn't just walk away from in the end.'

Amir had the grace to look a little shamefaced at that as he took her hand in his and led her to sit down on the bed beside him.

'That might have been true before I met you, but from the moment you walked into that airport lounge I knew I was lost. That's why I told my father that the wedding he had planned could never take place. What?' he questioned, looking down into her upturned face, seeing her bewilderment. 'What did I say?'

'You told your father that the arranged marriage was off?'

Amir nodded his dark head, his expression sombre.

'I told Aisha too. She's a lovely girl, very sweet, very attractive, but I knew that to me she could only ever be second-best. She would never be you. She deserved better than that. She deserved someone who could love her as the one and only person for them.'

'And you did this when I'd already gone? When you thought I'd left you? You risked your father's approval? The kingdom—for me?'

'I had no choice. You were the only woman I could ever feel this way about. But...'

Suddenly his expression lightened, the sensual lips curving up into a smile.

'I knew I was going to get you back. I *had* to get you back. That's why I made sure you were sent here.'

'I would never have gone, you know, if I'd read your note properly.' Lydia's voice was soft, her eyes glistening with tears at the memory.

'I only thought there was one page. I didn't read the second one until now.'

Amir's smile grew, and the eyes that looked down into hers were touched with a teasing light.

'I had already rung my father to say that I couldn't go through with the arranged marriage. I thought you would have guessed—number twenty-four,' he prompted when she still looked bemused.

'Number twenty-four?'

Gropingly, she tried to recall what the magazine article had said.

'Number twenty-four—"he takes you somewhere really special... Perhaps he has an extra-special proposal in mind?"'

'You...?'

'I was going to propose to you that night. That and your birthday were the only stages we hadn't covered. That was why I wanted you to wear the special dress. I was going to take you out and…'

Suddenly he astonished her by getting up, her hand still in his.

'And I was going to go down on one knee…'

His gaze fixed intently on her, he suited action to the words. Lydia could only watch, her heart thudding wildly in her breast.

'And I was going to say—Lydia, love of my heart, light of my life, would you make me the happiest man in the world by agreeing to marry me?'

'Oh, Amir, yes! Of course the answer's yes.'

The kiss that followed was long and deeply passionate, so intense that it left them both breathing raggedly. Looking into the darkness of Amir's eyes, Lydia knew that her future was sealed and that she would never be lonely again.

And as Amir gathered her up onto the bed beside him and began to slide the black silk of the *abaya* from her willing body, she had just one thought left in her head.

'If that was the something extra special, then just what did you have in mind for my birthday?'

'Can't you guess?'

Amir paused for one moment to smile into her eyes that shone with love for him.

'Your birthday, my love, was—is—to be the day that you become my bride.'

Lydia's answering smile said it all. She couldn't have been happier. Couldn't have wanted anything more in her life.

'Perfect,' she sighed. 'Just perfect.'

And as she gave herself up to his passion she knew that was how it would be for the rest of her days.

Modern Romance™
...seduction and
passion guaranteed

Tender Romance™
...love affairs that
last a lifetime

Sensual Romance™
...sassy, sexy and
seductive

Blaze
...sultry days and
steamy nights

Medical Romance™
...medical drama on
the pulse

Historical Romance™
...rich, vivid and
passionate

29 new titles every month.

*With all kinds of Romance for
every kind of mood...*

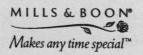

MILLS & BOON®

Makes any time special™

MAT4

MIRANDA LEE

Secrets & Sins revealed

SEDUCED BY HER BODYGUARD AND STALKED BY A STRANGER...

Available from 15th March 2002

FREE!

2 Books
and a surprise gift!

We would like to take this opportunity to thank you for reading this Mills & Boon® book by offering you the chance to take TWO more specially selected titles from the Modern Romance™ series absolutely FREE! We're also making this offer to introduce you to the benefits of the Reader Service™—

- ★ FREE home delivery
- ★ FREE gifts and competitions
- ★ FREE monthly Newsletter
- ★ Books available before they're in the shops
- ★ Exclusive Reader Service discount

Accepting these FREE books and gift places you under no obligation to buy; you may cancel at any time, even after receiving your free shipment. Simply complete your details below and return the entire page to the address below. **You don't even need a stamp!**

YES! Please send me 2 free Modern Romance books and a surprise gift. I understand that unless you hear from me, I will receive 4 superb new titles every month for just £2.49 each, postage and packing free. I am under no obligation to purchase any books and may cancel my subscription at any time. The free books and gift will be mine to keep in any case.

P2ZEB

Ms/Mrs/Miss/Mr ....Initials..
BLOCK CAPITALS PLEASE

Surname..

Address..

....

....Postcode ....

Send this whole page to:
UK: The Reader Service, FREEPOST CN81, Croydon, CR9 3WZ
EIRE: The Reader Service, PO Box 4546, Kilcock, County Kildare (stamp required)